## MARRIAGE CONTRACT

Party of the first part: Marcus Davenport

I promise to give Rachel a child to love and all the money she could possibly want. I will treat this marriage like a business arrangement and not involve my emotions—no matter how much I enjoy marital bliss.

Party of the second part: Rachel Vanden Ross

I promise to be the mother of Marcus's child, keep the home fires burning and make no demands on his affections—even though I yearn to ease his hurt and teach him how to love again.

Please address questions and book requests to: Silhouette Reader Service
U.S.: 3010 Walden Ave., P.O. Box 1325, Buffalo, NY 14269
Canadian: P.O. Box 609, Fort Erie, Ont. L2A 5X3

Solution: Wedding

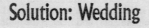

# SUZANNE CAREY

# A MOST CONVENIENT MARRIAGE

Published by Silhouette Books
**America's Publisher of Contemporary Romance**

SILHOUETTE BOOKS
300 East 42nd St.,
New York, N.Y. 10017

ISBN 0-373-30144-8

A MOST CONVENIENT MARRIAGE

Copyright © 1989 by Verna Carey

Celebrity Wedding Certificates published by permission of
Donald Ray Pounders from *Celebrity Wedding Ceremonies*.

This edition published by arrangement with Harlequin Books S.A.

® and TM are trademarks of Harlequin Books S.A., used under license.
Trademarks indicated with ® are registered in the United States Patent and
Trademark Office, the Canadian Trade Marks Office and in other countries.

Printed in U.S.A.

## A Letter from the Author

Dear Reader,

Among the many books I've written *A Most Convenient Marriage* has always been one of my favorites. In part, I suppose, that's because of the romantic setting: London, Paris and the wildly picturesque Breton coast. But it's not the only reason. The real clincher for me is the almost painful longing for true love and emotional commitment on the part of widowed, betrayed Rachel Vanden Ross and her problematic, emotionally burned hero, Marcus Davenport. It positively pervades the story, even as the events that unfold blaze with sensual fireworks. Reading it again for the first time after almost nine years, I could feel it like a physical ache.

I can relate to it better in retrospect. Since writing *A Most Convenient Marriage,* I have been widowed, too. After grieving for what seemed like forever, and subsequently dating a number of what I call Y.B.I.B.'s (short for "You blew it, buddy!"), I was commitment-shy and skeptical. Yet I ached for the kind of one-on-one relationship that makes life worth living and brings out the best in us.

Much to my surprise, just as Marcus did for Rachel, someone wonderful appeared when the time was right. Thanks to him, and the terrific life we've built together, the "Happy Clam" sign is lit again above my writing desk. Here's hoping your "Happy Clam" sign is getting a workout, too.

With warm regards,

Suzanne Carey

For The Snog, with all my love

# Chapter One

It was the kind of day that could be rendered in watercolors, a late March day with the trees still bare and clouds scudding across the sky. Crocuses carpeted the lush green lawn of St. James Park with their tender yellow, white and lavender petals. Looking at the lake with its flocks of ducks and the crowd of nannies pushing prams along its banks, Rachel Vanden Ross was reminded of a Maurice Prendergast painting in New York City's Metropolitan Museum.

She, Prendergast and the Metropolitan were American. The park with its nannies and rosy-cheeked babies, on the other hand, was British. Surrounding it on all sides was London, and Rachel was glad of that. She'd fallen in love with the city as a girl of ten when she'd accompanied her father on one of his crusades. Now, as a working resident for most of the three months that had passed since her husband's funeral, she felt free for the first time since childhood.

Both her former selves—the mousy young woman who'd served as her evangelist father's dedicated assistant, and the poised, long-suffering wife of businessman and political candidate Desmond Ross—had ceased to exist.

After twenty-nine years, the real Rachel had finally emerged. She was a clean-scrubbed, modest and youthful-looking widow with a heavy plait of dark hair that hung down her back. No longer required to impress anyone, she dressed for comfort. Today she was wearing a sweater and slim khaki-colored trousers topped by a raincoat. Quietly resolved not to be dominated again by someone like her father or shamed by a husband's cheating, she'd given up on men. Henceforth, she would concentrate on building the successful art career she'd always wanted.

A check for two hundred and fifty pounds was tucked safely inside her wallet and bore witness that her foot was on the first rung of the ladder. Drawn on the account of Trewitt Galleries, 18 Dover Street, W1, it represented her first sale, a study of working-class waifs in London's impoverished East End. She'd taken an extralong lunch hour to pick it up, and she'd experienced a distinct thrill of pleasure when Ian Trewitt had placed it in her hand.

Why then, she asked herself, did the nannies and their charges make her feel something akin to sadness? She'd long since come to terms with Des's inability to give her a child and his refusal to adopt one. Now that she'd chosen the single life, her childless state would be permanent. It couldn't be allowed to matter that her heart went out to every sweet-faced toddler or that motherhood had figured strongly in her youthful hopes and dreams.

Closing her sketchbook, Rachel relinquished her bench to catch a red double-decker bus back to Fleet Street. She worked as a commercial artist at Elite Ltd., an international credit-banking firm that controlled a luxury-hotel chain and one of Europe's fastest growing airlines. In an extraordinary piece of luck, she'd managed to secure a work visa through Tom Clancy, her late husband's campaign manager. Shortly after Des's funeral she'd told Tom about her wish to live and work in London, never guessing he'd be the key to realizing her dream. To her surprise, Tom's brother-in-law, a native Briton, headed up Elite's advertising department. After a quick trip to London she'd been hired.

Now that I'm here I plan to make the most of my opportunity, Rachel vowed, sliding into her seat on the bus and balancing her sketchbook on her knees. Admittedly her quick drawings of the upper-class children and their starchy but devoted nurses had a certain charm, but they weren't the sort of thing she hoped would make her reputation. On the easel in her tiny Chelsea flat was a painting similar in style to the one she'd sold today. Following her work that afternoon on a page layout for Elite's advertising department, she'd turn her attention to the painting again.

The bus was crowded with salesgirls, office clerks and eccentric-looking elderly types who carried umbrellas and wore hand-knit sweaters under their rain gear. Just ahead of Rachel sat a discreetly amorous couple. The couple made her feel as pensive as the children had. Turning away, she gazed out the window at the passing vista of Somerset House and King's College, watching the soberly dressed barristers who frequented the Inns of Court in their short wigs and Puritan collars.

Try as she would she couldn't seem to avoid witnessing romantic displays of affection. Walking the half block from her bus stop in the heart of London's publishing district, she slowed her pace as she recognized the tall dark-haired man getting out of a limousine in front of Elite Ltd.'s imposing plate-glass entrance.

Well, she acknowledged softly. If it isn't Marcus Davenport—a legend in his own time, whether you read the business news or the scandal sheets. She thought wryly that Elite's attractive chief executive was probably a legend *between* the sheets, as well. Never mind that some of the photographs showing him with stunning women were taken at corporate events or charity balls. The women gazing at him so adoringly didn't look as if they had business on their minds.

Rachel had seen him around the offices before, of course, glimpsing him at a distance as he'd prowled the halls of his multimillion-dollar conglomerate. Now with the opportunity to observe him up close, she was reluctantly forced to admit that the broad-shouldered tycoon was one of the best looking men she'd ever seen.

He was in his late thirties, she guessed. And out-fitted by the best Savile Row tailors.

For a moment he appeared to glance in her direction. Then he was leaning back into the car to kiss a stunning woman goodbye. Rachel caught sight of his companion's smooth blond hair and aristocratic profile. Hands elegantly gloved in gray suede framed Davenport's face.

Averting her eyes, Rachel found herself facing a wrinkled dame in shabby black who was hawking nosegays. Doubtless it was an illusion, but the old woman seemed to guess at her uncomfortable mix of emotions. It's true, Rachel conceded silently, digging out the price of a bunch of daffodils. I may have chosen celibacy as the lesser of two evils, but there's still a part of me that would like to be in that woman's place.

As she turned back toward the building with her flowers, Marcus Davenport was stepping away from the curb. "See you later," a husky female voice called after him.

"Not tonight, ducks." A slightly lopsided grin served notice that his use of the cockney expression was just a charming affectation. "I won't be able to make your party," he added in a casual tone. "Business, you know."

As the sleek silver-gray Rolls pulled away, Rachel tried to imagine the woman's disappointment. *I wonder if they had lunch, or something more intimate,* she thought as she followed Davenport into the building. *Maybe it was both.* Whatever the case she doubted it implied any commitment on Davenport's part.

The nosegay of daffodils, so impulsively purchased, made a bright spot of color above Rachel's worktable that afternoon. Glancing at them now and then and tapping her foot to soft music from a portable radio, she focused on the ad she was creating. An alluring promotion for Air Anglia, it would feature a pastel sketch of a woman reclining in an openweave hammock. One tanned shapely leg would spill over the hammock's edge as the woman stirred sugary Jamaican sand with her toes.

"Miss Vanden Ross?" An unfamiliar voice broke her concentration.

Rachel looked up, frowning slightly. A thin brownhaired man with a hawk nose and glasses was standing beside her worktable. "Actually, it's *Mrs.* Ross," she corrected.

"Oh, right. Sorry." The man extended his hand. "Permit me to introduce myself. I'm Alan Travers, Mr. Davenport's assistant."

Her frown deepened. "How d'you do?" she murmured, wiping her fingers on a cloth so she could offer him a grave handshake.

The brown-haired man smiled as if he wished to set her at ease. "Pleased to make your acquaintance," he said. "I suppose you're wondering why I sought you out. Actually, Mr. Davenport would like a word with you."

Initially Rachel had been puzzled, but now she regarded him with something approaching alarm. "I'm not being fired, am I?" she asked. "Or sacked, as I believe you call it here?"

"Good heavens, no." Alan Travers's smile widened. "Perhaps we'd better let Mr. Davenport explain. I say, would you like to freshen up a bit? You've got a smudge of that attractive sky-blue color on your chin."

Despite the extraordinary drift of their conversation, they were speaking in clearly audible tones. Rachel sensed that work at some of the nearby tables had ceased.

"Yes, I think I would," she agreed hastily.

Taking off her smock, she picked up her purse and hurried off to the austere white-tiled sanctuary of the ladies' room. So I'm going to meet the great man, she thought, unable to suppress a small shiver of excitement. The feeling was quickly replaced by dismay when she confronted her reflection. I *would* wear slacks and this dratted sweater, she sighed, smoothing down a faded pink mohair pullover that had seen better days.

A closer look in the mirror confirmed the presence of blue chalk on her face. Dampening a tissue, she wiped it clean and evaluated her hair. Wind and the ravages of the day had disarranged her neat braid. In fact, several naturally wavy strands had completely escaped.

Sighing again, she undid the plait and brushed her dark tresses vigorously until they shone. The only makeup in her purse was a light pink lipstick. Applying it, she took critical stock of her dark-fringed blue eyes, well-shaped brows and flawless complexion, quite oblivious to their natural beauty.

"Well," she said with a fatalistic shrug, "that's the best I can do. He'll have to take me as I am."

The fact that she'd been summoned by the company president didn't sink in completely until she and Alan Travers were being whisked upstairs in the express elevator. Despite her resolve to stay calm, an uneasy sensation settled in the pit of her stomach.

As they passed through the executive foyer, Rachel was able to garner only fleeting impressions. She noted thick gray carpet, recessed lighting and a bunching, powerful sculpture that might be a Henry Moore original atop its rosewood plinth. With a nod at Rachel's escort, the sleek fortyish receptionist waved them past. Opening one of the tall paneled doors to Davenport's private office, Alan Travers motioned for her to precede him. A moment later she was facing Davenport himself across the vast polished surface of his desk.

Deferentially Alan Travers made the proper introductions. The tall dark-haired man who'd claimed her attention so effortlessly a few hours before got to his feet. Walking around the desk to meet her, he extended his hand.

Rachel offered her own in reply. His grip was firm and sure, surprisingly full of feeling. It was as if a small jolt of electricity passed between them at the touch.

''Thank you for coming, Mrs. Ross,'' he said in his deep, cultivated voice.

She stared at him, half-mesmerized. Her sensation was one of drowning in blue eyes that were the deep rich shade of a storm at sea. Beneath the intensity of his gaze, her own wavered. She found herself focusing on details—his sooty-black lashes, the way his brows slanted upward toward the bridge of his nose, a perceived trace of a continental accent.

Though she stood in awe of Marcus Davenport's position, she'd expected nothing more complicated from him socially than the negligent charm of a playboy. But though this man exuded more natural sex appeal than she'd ever encountered, he was far less accessible than she'd imagined. Keen and curious, his eyes gave away no secrets.

If he thought it strange that she continued to stand there without speaking, he was too well-bred to say so. With a reluctant air, he tore his gaze from hers and rested it on his subordinate. "Thank you, Alan," he said. "You might have Mrs. Billingsham send in some tea."

"Yes, sir." With a reassuring smile for Rachel, Alan Travers left the room.

She barely noted his departure. Returning his attention to her, Marcus Davenport smoothly established their rapport. No wonder the tabloids label him "England's most eligible catch," she thought, taking in his powerful build, firmly chiseled features and generous, uneven mouth. His compelling good looks guaranteed that he'd be the gossipmongers' darling even if he lived like a monk and lost every cent in the stock market.

But it wasn't just his appearance or obvious warm-blooded sensuality that so intrigued Rachel as she stood with her hand captured in his. Rather, it was an added dimension—a kind of star quality that had more to do with decisiveness and personal strength than glamour. Stubbornness, passion and humor were clearly etched in the lines around his mouth. A sixth sense told her he was fond of risk-taking, a man who delighted in achieving his ends by unorthodox means.

Yet her first impression that he erected defenses held, and at the moment not a chink of vulnerability was showing. Here's a man, she decided, who guards his innermost thoughts as if they were treasures. A man who doesn't lightly bestow his affection. His blond friend in the limousine is in for some heartaches. In fact, he'd be quite a challenge for anyone....

Suddenly aware of the direction her thoughts were taking, Rachel tethered herself on a short leash. Davenport's love life doesn't concern you, she told herself in no uncertain terms. You're not in the market for a man, even one with his sterling qualifications. What an idiot you must seem, woolgathering this way.

She withdrew her hand. "It's a pleasure to meet you, Mr. Davenport," she said crisply, declining to apologize for her awkward behavior. "I'll admit I'm wondering why you sent for me. As a very junior commercial artist on your advertising staff, I doubt I'm the sort of person you usually summon into your presence."

Davenport's mouth curved slightly. Perhaps he liked the way that, once she'd found her voice, she used it to come directly to the point. "Please," he said. "Call me Marcus. You're right, of course. But one must stay in touch with one's employees, don't you think?"

Tacitly noting his avoidance of her question, Rachel allowed him to settle her on a luxurious sofa covered in dusky-blue velvet. It had been strategically placed to take advantage of a stunning view. Brooding in the first wreaths of afternoon mist, the

Thames and its south bank stretched off into the distance beyond a floor-to-ceiling wall of glass.

A moment later Mrs. Billingsham appeared with their tea. Taking his place beside her, Rachel's host dismissed the secretary and poured for them with a practiced hand. "You're the girl I saw on the street, aren't you?" he asked, catching her off guard as he passed her a fragile teacup, filled with the steaming dark brew. "The one with the daffodils?"

Rachel couldn't hide her surprise. "I can't believe you noticed me."

"Ah, but I did. Your hair is different, isn't it?"

"I had it in a braid before."

The guarded look in his eyes relaxed a little. "I prefer it this way," he said. "Loose and curling around your face."

His intensely personal remark evoked that odd tingly feeling again. Rachel strove to quell it. "That's not why you asked me here, is it?" she said. "Noticing me on the street, I mean."

For the first time, Marcus Davenport really smiled, and she was struck by the boyish air it gave his face. "Actually, no," he admitted. "At the time, I didn't realize..." Breaking off, he regarded her for a moment without speaking. "Mind if I ask you a few questions?" he said at last.

Rachel hesitated. Too many inquiries from strangers—particularly about her father or Des—were among the unpleasantries she'd come to London to avoid. Yet anonymity seemed to evade her even here.

He appeared to take her silence for assent. "You've been with us nearly three months now," he said. "You're a widow. And childless. The only child of world-renowned evangelist Luther Vanden."

Rachel stared. "Right so far."

He leaned back a little. "Actually," he said, "you used to sing on Dr. Vanden's television programs. You traveled abroad with him, too, serving as his press secretary and booking agent. Of course, you were less active in that regard after you married... the man of his choice, I might add, cable television executive and political conservative Desmond Ross. I imagine that's because Ross required your services in his bid for the U.S. House of Representatives—"

"It was the Senate."

She corrected him almost absently. Is he going to describe my life in detail, she wondered? Explain how Des suffered a fatal heart attack in the arms of his last mistress? Or compliment me on how well I bore up through the funeral? If Marcus Davenport does this much research on everyone who crosses his path, he must be a formidable business opponent.

"Tell me how it was, living in your father's shadow," he suggested.

Something in his manner made her want to do just that; yet, she'd been trained to protect the men in her life—whether they deserved it or not.

"What do you want to know?" she asked warily. "Surely you don't expect me to tell tales out of school."

He smiled again. "Loyalty's an admirable quality, Rachel. I wasn't testing yours. I'm just curious what life was like for you, growing up under those circumstances. Most especially after your mother died."

"Lonely." The single word was out before she could stop it. "Oh, there were always people around," she continued. "Some of them were even my age. But I didn't have much time for friendships. We were always traveling. When Mom died I was fifteen. I was expected to take her place... live up to Dad's impossibly high standards—"

"They weren't yours?"

She shrugged. "Not always. I didn't feel as devout, as self-effacing as he wanted me to be. Today my value system's my own, though I try to incorporate the good things my father taught me. Above all, I prize my independence, something he hasn't yet understood."

Marcus Davenport nodded. His capable-looking hands framed his teacup.

"You ask how it was, traveling with Dad," she went on, rewarding his silence. "Sometimes I just went through the motions. I'd try my best to play whatever part he wanted, while my real self escaped in imagination. You see, I had other plans for my life—"

"Like being an artist?"

No doubt he knew about her affiliation with Trewitt Galleries, as well. "Yes," she admitted. "Art was always my dream. That and getting married, raising a family. I used to picture myself painting on an easel in some big old North Carolina farmhouse kitchen, with a baby cradled against my shoulder."

A half-hidden spark leapt into his eyes at that. Abruptly breaking off visual contact, she looked down at her hands. "I can't believe I'm talking to you this way," she confessed. "You're a busy man. Surely you didn't invite me to your office to discuss my girlhood fantasies."

"In a way, I did."

There was a small silence, and Rachel felt he was about to explain what was on his mind. A moment later he appeared to think better of it.

"My objective at this point is simply to get to know you," he said, as if he felt some kind of accounting was necessary. "I promise to share the reason for that...soon. Unfortunately, it's almost quitting time. If you're to return home and change—"

Rachel frowned, feeling as if she'd missed something. "I'm not sure I understand."

"Forgive me." A rueful expression played about the corners of his mouth. "It seems I've taken the cart before the horse, as they say in your quaint Yankee expression."

"*Put* the cart before the horse." Stubbornly she awaited his explanation.

As if he were seeking temporary relief from some hidden stress, Marcus Davenport lit a cigarette. "The fact is, I may have a business proposal for you," he said. "I thought we might explore the possibility over dinner tonight. If you're free, perhaps I could send my car for you about seven?"

Rachel's eyes widened. Though it made no sense whatsoever, apparently she was the "business" that had prompted him to refuse his gorgeous blonde.

"I suppose you already know my address?" she asked.

"Actually, yes." His eyes gleamed in appreciation of the left-handed compliment. "It's 56 Upper Cheyne Row, the garret flat. Well, what do you say, Rachel? Will you dine with me tonight?"

Faced with the need to answer him, Rachel hesitated. "Are we discussing dinner at your house?" she asked. "If so, I wouldn't feel comfortable—"

His smile broadened. "What was that you said about your father's values? No, don't explain. I find your attitude extremely refreshing. In any case, the idea of dining in never crossed my mind. Will Mirabelle be all right instead?"

Quite casually he named one of the city's most chic and expensive restaurants. Ah, for the privileges of money, she thought. And an ethical system that would let you take full advantage of them. But she didn't really envy her wealthy employer. As Luther

Vanden's daughter, she'd been taught to think in terms of good works and achievement, not self-gratification.

Yet it was impossible not to smile at him. "Mira-belle will be fine," she said.

"Good," he replied.

For one heart-stopping moment then, he squeezed her hand. She had the strong impression of being drawn into something so absorbing, so all-consuming that it would alter the very fabric of her life. But that was nonsense, of course. What harm could there be in having dinner with the boss, she rationalized, bidding him good afternoon. He seemed a perfect gentleman despite his reputation.

Her prosaic assessment of the afternoon's events notwithstanding, there was a sparkle in Rachel's eyes and a spring in her step that had been missing before her tea with Marcus Davenport. Her colleagues in the art department didn't fail to note it. Besieged with questions, she tried to remain polite but firmly noncommittal. Gathering up her things as quickly as she could, she took refuge in the rush-hour stream of employees leaving the building.

It was only after finding a seat on the crowded Chelsea bus that she began asking herself some serious questions. What kind of business proposal can Marcus Davenport possibly have in mind? she wondered. I haven't been at Elite long enough to distinguish myself.

He could scarcely regard her as a potential investor. If he'd taken the trouble to check her background as thoroughly as she supposed, he must know she'd signed over most of Des's assets to the children of his first marriage. Her salary, necessary to meet the expenses of daily living, and her modest cushion of savings could hardly interest him.

She was slightly ashamed for thinking he might hope to use her as a conduit to her father. He may be a playboy, she thought, but you have no reason to suspect him of ulterior motives. With his credentials, he doesn't need a go-between. Dad would never rebuff a potential contributor of Marcus Davenport's means.

The only other possible explanation made even less sense. It was ridiculous to speculate that her employer's allusion to a business proposal was his way of seducing her into an after-hours fling—not with women like the elegant blonde in her limousine clamoring for his attention. The whole thing's a mystery to me, Rachel concluded, flexing the day's stiffness out of her shoulders. I can't wait to get some answers tonight.

Her curiosity would have known no bounds if she could have eavesdropped outside Marcus Davenport's office at that very moment. Holding a file marked ''Rachel Vanden Ross,'' Elite's chief executive left off pacing before his magnificent view to fix Alan Travers with a penetrating look.

"You were right," he admitted, a hint of reluctance in his voice. "She's old-fashioned, intelligent and surprisingly nice looking."

Alan had dropped the formalities to which he'd adhered so rigorously in Rachel's presence. "In that case, I don't see why you're hesitating," he replied. "You said it yourself, she's everything you wanted."

Marcus stood with his back to the windows. Behind him the lights of London were winking as mist crept in from the river, forming a translucent veil that partially obscured the smoking chimneys of Bankside power station.

"Everything," he agreed, his strong features lost in shadow. "And yet, I wonder.... Something tells me she'll turn out to be more than I bargained for."

# Chapter Two

Standing in her stocking feet before the cubbyhole that served her as a closet, Rachel considered a sapphire-blue silk jacquard cocktail dress. With its ruffled neckline and sleeves designed to be worn slightly off the shoulder, it seemed too frivolous for a weeknight dinner appointment. Yet her wardrobe didn't offer many options. Before leaving for London, she'd sold or given away most of the clothes she'd worn during her marriage, the way a butterfly sheds its cocoon before trying its wings.

I'd be hard-pressed to come up with more suitable attire, Rachel thought, slipping the silk from its padded hanger. Then she smiled. The odds were this would be her one chance to dine in style with Marcus Davenport. She might as well look her best.

Twenty minutes later she was positioning the blue gown's sleeves as modestly as possible and fastening her mother's cameo necklace around her neck. In deference to the occasion, she'd dabbed on a bit of perfume and swept her hair into an Edwardian-style pouf that left several mahogany-dark strands curling about her face.

Surveying her handiwork on the small, partially blackened mirror over her pantry sink, Rachel wasn't impressed. *I look lamentably innocent and clean scrubbed—as if I still sing in the choir at Dad's first church in Greensboro, North Carolina,* she thought. *I can just imagine the headlines if the tabloids get hold of this: "Eligible Catch Baby-sits."*

Just then the downstairs bell rang shrilly. It was followed by the sound of voices—one deep and masculine, the other female, elderly and a trifle querulous, belonging to Grace Tweedt, her landlady.

Pushing back the lace curtain that hung at her front window, Rachel saw a black Daimler parked at the curb. Its engine was running. Powerful headlights pierced the evening mist as the uniformed driver lounged against one well-polished fender.

Rather than ask his chauffeur to deliver her to the restaurant, Elite's chief executive had decided to call for her himself. A moment later she tensed at his quick footsteps. He was rapping on her door and she was opening it, stepping back to murmur a soft hello.

In his evening clothes, black overcoat and white silk muffler, Marcus Davenport looked the epitome of a sophisticated man-about-town—handsome, rich and a trifle racy, a predatory financier playing at being civilized.

"Good evening, Rachel," he said. Indigo eyes that held little trace of the afternoon's warmth raked her up and down, finally registering approval. "Since you're ready, what do you say we dispense with the formalities and depart?"

"I'll just get my coat." Rachel spoke the words a trifle despairingly. Only moments before, she'd realized that she possessed no suitable wrap. But he didn't seem to notice the contrast between her tan poplin raincoat and his own faultless garments.

Grace Tweedt's curiosity was tangible as they went down to the car, but Marcus seemed oblivious to the older woman's stares. He appeared lost in contemplation as he settled Rachel against the plush upholstery of his expensive automobile and got in beside her.

Barely glancing back, Marcus's chauffeur shifted gears and set off for Curzon Street. As far as he's concerned, I'm just a walk-on in a cast of thousands, Rachel thought. Stealing a look at Marcus's aloof profile, she speculated again about the purpose of their meeting. The idea that they could have business dealings of any sort was still so preposterous she couldn't imagine what he had in mind.

Mirabelle's maître d' greeted them with a deference laced with familiarity, making it plain Marcus
was a valued customer of long standing. Though the
restaurant was somewhat crowded, he ushered them
immediately to a secluded table screened by bloom-
ing hibiscus and potted palms.

Their progress across the softly lit peach-and-green
dining room between barley-sugar-twist columns and
elegantly set tables was marked by smiles and waves
from several other patrons. One of them, a ravish-
ing redhead, made no attempt to hide her keen interest in Rachel's identity. Old flame number three
thousand and three, Rachel thought, amused even as
she suppressed a small stab of jealousy.

The à la carte menu she received didn't quote
prices. Polite to a fault and doubtless aware she was
in an unfamiliar setting, Marcus offered to order for
her. Issuing his instructions without giving the
printed selections more than a cursory glance, he
emerged from his thoughts to smile. "I must say you
look quite lovely tonight," he said. "With your hair
arranged that way, you remind me of the first photograph I ever saw of you."

Had he studied various likenesses of her, then?
And if so, why? Rachel's delicate winged brows
arched slightly as she waited for him to elaborate.

"I was in the States on business last December
when *The New York Times* carried an account of
your husband's funeral," he said. "The story re-
ferred briefly to the circumstances surrounding his

death. In the picture that accompanied it, you were standing at the graveside with your father and Ross's two grown sons. Ross's ex-wife was there, too, and apparently you didn't object to that. I remember thinking how poised and self-contained you seemed, how thoroughly capable you were of handling what must have been a very difficult situation."

Rachel dismissed the compliment with a shrug. The sommelier had arrived with their wine, offering the first sample from the bottle to Marcus, and she withheld any response for a moment.

"Actually, I was numb," she admitted when the man had poured for them and left the table. "I won't pretend I enjoyed the notoriety or the public disgrace that accompanied my husband's death."

Marcus nodded. "My ex-wife, actress Deirdre Martin, was unfaithful to me. I know how it feels. Mind telling me why you and Ross didn't have any children?"

Offering just a single tantalizing glimpse at his past, Marcus had shifted the focus to her again. There seemed to be no end to his interest in her private affairs.

"On the supposition you plan to justify this kind of third degree," she said, "I'll tell you. It had nothing to do with Des's, well, 'indiscretions.' He'd undergone an operation before our marriage, you see, and he wasn't able to father any more children. He didn't favor adoption. He already had his sons and they, apparently, were enough for him."

Marcus regarded her intently. "But were they enough for you?" he asked.

The query penetrated her innermost defenses. "If you've investigated me as thoroughly as I suspect you have," she replied with some asperity as two exquisitely presented servings of *huîtres à la champagne* arrived at their table, "you already know it wasn't. It's no secret that I wanted a baby of my own to love more than anything in the world."

With a gleam of what might have been secret satisfaction, Marcus changed the subject with the finesse of a diplomat. First they discussed her art and its portrayal of disadvantaged children, and then he moved on to his career. Their conversation didn't flag throughout a meal of *noix de veau aux cèpes*, rice and tiny flambéed carrots, finished off with a selection of cheeses and ruddy imported pears. To Rachel, his unique perspective on the company she worked for was fascinating. She particularly enjoyed hearing about the initial risky business venture he'd undertaken as a twenty-six-year-old.

Yet, entertaining as they were, his "war stories" didn't give her much insight into the private man. He probably doesn't reveal very much about himself unless it suits his purposes, she thought.

She was surprised a moment later when he lit an after-dinner cigarette and returned to the far more volatile topic of his personal life.

"I mentioned before that my ex-wife was unfaithful," he said, carefully noting her reaction. "But I didn't tell you the whole story."

If Rachel had learned anything from her father and Des, it was how to be a receptive listener. Leaning forward slightly in her chair, she encouraged him to continue.

"Though Deirdre didn't want children," he obliged, "mistakes happen. Despite her precautions, she became pregnant. And in due course we had a beautiful son.

"Jamie was three when we divorced. I was granted custody, though Deirdre had visitation. Because of her infidelity after Jamie's birth, she didn't get the handsome court settlement she'd expected. I suppose that's why she enlisted her latest lover's aid in faking a kidnapping scheme."

Pausing, he took a drag on his cigarette while Rachel tried to contain her astonishment and distress.

"During their attempt to return him without getting caught," Marcus added, "Jamie was struck by a car. He died soon after in hospital."

"Oh, no!" Her intention of keeping a safe emotional distance between them was forgotten as Rachel reached impulsively for his hand. "I'm so *sorry*," she whispered. "I know that doesn't help. My God . . . to have a child and then to lose him that way! It must be the worst thing that can happen to anyone in this world."

Marcus didn't answer. Yet for a moment he didn't shrug off her touch.

"Enough about my private sorrows," he said, breaking away as he glanced at his watch, a thin Patek Phillipe that gleamed luxuriously golden against his wrist. "If we hurry, we can just about make it to Gordon's before they close."

Shaken by his painful self-revelation and the brief moment of intimacy that had followed it, Rachel didn't protest. But she was brimming with speculation as he paid the bill. Clearly Marcus played both his business and personal lives close to the chest. He had to have a very good reason for revealing such a deep emotional hurt.

A brief ride through the Covent Garden district brought them to the Adelphi, an area Rachel recognized from a tour she'd taken during her first week in London. At that hour on a weeknight, the street where they halted was all but deserted. Advising his chauffeur to return in about an hour, Marcus helped her out of the car.

They stood facing a narrow, dimly lit passageway marked by sharply descending steps. Grim-looking eighteenth-century buildings loomed on either side, connected at the lower end of the alley by a massive stone gate.

Despite her usually adventurous spirit, Rachel hung back a little. "Your choice of entertainments doesn't look too promising," she remarked.

Marcus laughed. "Not to worry," he advised, guiding her steps on the damp, slippery pavement to a dingy unmarked entrance. "As a London institution, Gordon's is every bit as respectable as the Albert Memorial."

To her delight, hidden away in this unlikely corner of the city was a quintessential British drinking establishment. She noted with pleasure its abundance of antique leaded glass, oak wainscoting and worn, well-polished brass. Above the bar a thicket of bottles gleamed, picking up amber, burgundy and deep green reflections from a crackling fire. A handful of patrons stood at the bar or occupied a dozen or so tables that were lit with dripping wax candles.

Selecting a corner table set slightly apart from the others, Marcus settled Rachel in an oak-and-leather chair. The sherry he ordered wasn't poured ceremoniously from a bottle. Instead it flowed into their glasses from the spigot of a huge wooden keg.

"Thank you for the lovely dinner," Rachel said after they were served and Marcus lifted his glass in a silent toast. "In fact, for a very pleasant evening," she continued. "Yet I can't help wondering why you've said nothing about the business you mentioned this afternoon. Have you changed your mind for some reason? If not, I'm terribly curious."

"I haven't changed my mind." Tapping out his cigarette, Marcus took his time lighting it. "Actually," he said, exhaling a cloud of smoke, "our conversation has only firmed up my intent. If you'll hear me out, no matter how seemingly unconventional the idea I'm about to propose, I'll endeavor to explain.''

"All right." Seized with a thrill of anticipation, Rachel rested her chin on her hand.

For a moment her escort studied her without speaking before he began. "Last month I celebrated my thirty-eighth birthday. As I mentioned over dinner, I've managed to build up what most people would consider a substantial enterprise. Naturally half the pleasure of that's in the struggle to succeed. But any sense of accomplishment fades when there's nobody to come after you, benefit from what you've achieved. At one time I expected my son, Jamie, to inherit. But his death canceled those hopes.''

Rachel frowned. She could appreciate how he felt, but so far his explanation wasn't making much sense.

"You say you're thirty-eight," she mused. "That's hardly middle-aged. Certainly you can be expected to marry again.''

If her reference to middle age nettled him, he didn't show it. "Why *certainly*, Rachel?" he asked in a mild tone. "Does the same certainty apply to you?''

In light of her own determination to stay single, she couldn't argue.

"If my investigation of your background is correct," he said, "you were very disappointed in your marriage to Ross. When circumstances set you free, you decided not to become entangled again. As a result you suffer frustrated maternal longings. . . ."

Rachel winced. "You've got me there," she admitted reluctantly, her voice scarcely above a whisper. "I've already confessed how much I wanted a baby."

"You needn't apologize for your feelings. Like you, I was burned and I'm disinclined to remarry, as well. Yet I, too, want a child. If I am to be a father again, marriage seems the best option.

"That's why I asked Alan to evaluate various women for me, with the object of finding the best possible mother for my baby. He began with staff partly because that was easier. You may recall Elite employees sign a waiver allowing the company to perform background checks."

*Began with staff? Background checks?* Suddenly beginning to see a possible connection, Rachel felt as if her head were whirling. "Bu . . . but that's barbarous!" she exclaimed.

"I don't see why." Calmly he knocked the ash from his cigarette. "Having a child is one of the most important things one can do in one's life, both from the standpoint of genetic survival and that of personal gratification. It seems to me the truly barbaric way of going about it would be to leave things to chance."

Though he hadn't said anything, Rachel was beginning to get the strong impression he planned to recruit her for his outlandish scheme. If he's serious about this, she thought, choking back her dismay and anger, then he's a chauvinist of the worst sort—a man who doesn't mind using women as objects to attain his own ends.

Torn between the urge to flee and a burning desire to slap his face, she was overwhelmed by morbid curiosity. "Go ahead," she dared him, tight-lipped. "Tell me what kind of woman you're looking for. Wild horses couldn't drag me from this spot."

Elite's dark-haired chief had the grace to look slightly abashed. Yet his answer was in no way a tentative one. "The mother of my child," he said, "must be intelligent, healthy and refined, as well as reasonably good-looking, preferably with coloring that matches my own—"

Involuntarily Rachel's hand flew to her cheek. With her hair color and complexion, she realized she matched his requirements to perfection.

"She must also be willing to marry me," he was saying. "So my son or daughter will grow up with the benefit of both parents."

Stubbornly she fought back the urge to tears. "You can't have it both ways," she reminded him. "A moment ago you said you were disinclined to marry."

"And so I am. I consider matrimony in the conventional sense, where romance and love are supposed to play a part, completely out of the question. I don't intend to put myself in a woman's hands to that extent again."

"Then I don't see how—"

"It's quite simple, really. Though she must be a warm-natured, caring individual who will make the best of mothers, my wife must agree to make no demands on my affection."

At that, Rachel's mouth fell open in astonishment.

"Of course," he hastened to add, "the child will be conceived in the usual fashion. Where two healthy parents are involved, I see no reason to entrust the matter to test-tube tiddlywinks. But once the deed is done the next Mrs. Davenport won't be required to grant me any further bedroom privileges."

"You're joking!" To Rachel, the kind of marriage he was describing was no marriage at all.

"On the contrary." His eyes narrowing, Marcus gauged her reaction. "I fully intend that my wife and I shall be free to lead our separate lives," he said. "She must agree not to interfere with my life away from her, provided I'm discreet. In return, she'll have the same latitude, plus a child to love, the opportunity to pursue any career she wishes and all the money she could possibly want—to spend or give away, just as she chooses."

Try as she would to stanch them, Rachel's eyes filled with tears. "Oh, splendid!" she burst out. "Do you also plan to offer the lucky woman paid vacations? Life insurance benefits? Workmen's compensation?"

Too upset to say anything further, she tried to compose herself. It hurt to admit that his wild idea made a perverse kind of sense. The way it dovetailed with her own needs didn't bear thinking about.

She certainly had to hand it to him for taking the practical approach. Faced with the same dilemma that haunted her, he hadn't resigned himself to childlessness. Instead, he would hire a brood mare cum nursemaid—not just for the nine months it took to bring a child into the world, but on a permanent basis. To work, the scheme would require compartmentalization of the highest order, yet he seemed fully capable of arranging his life that way.

A woman had hurt and humiliated him; ergo, he'd feel nothing more complicated than lust for a woman again. As a bit of added insurance, he'd choose for his wife a woman like herself—someone naive, wholesome and devoid of glamour who wouldn't engender any unwanted attachments. With the ideal family tucked away at home, Marcus Davenport would be free to escape any form of emotional commitment.

Convinced she was a candidate to keep his home fires burning, Rachel found his litany of inducements highly offensive. If he thinks money and guarantees of latitude could persuade me to go along with such a plan, she thought, he *hasn't* done his homework. I'm not that kind of person!

Besides his attitude toward marriage itself was an affront to her. Despite her own unhappy experience, she considered matrimony a tender, sacred partnership. His callous relegation of it to business-deal status shocked her to the core.

Well, good luck to him, she thought fiercely, reaching for her purse. I pity the poor woman who accepts his offer. All the benefits in the world won't compensate for her embarrassment and heartache.

Just then, the barkeep approached to warn them Gordon's was closing. Slipping him a five-pound note, Marcus returned to their discussion.

"Perhaps I should mention there's a catch or two," he said, ignoring her strong hints that she'd heard enough. "For one thing, I shall require a prenuptial agreement assigning custody to me in the event of a divorce. Also, my wife must agree to end our marriage amicably if, after two years, she hasn't conceived. In that event, of course, she'd be handsomely compensated."

Did he plan to run a whole gamut of women, like some ancient potentate, until one of them produced an heir? To Rachel's chagrin, she realized it probably wouldn't come to that. Marcus Davenport had already sired one son under adverse circumstances and would probably have little difficulty getting a woman pregnant.

The thought of how easily he could strike the spark of new life within her stabbed at Rachel's consciousness. Looking at him across the table, she had little doubt they'd make a beautiful baby together.

Angry at herself for even thinking such thoughts, she struggled for words. "What you're contemplating is sheer madness," she told him, her voice sharper than she'd intended. "Marriages of convenience went out with the nineteenth century."

Marcus remained unperturbed. "Perhaps it's time they came back into fashion," he said. "Today most marriages end in divorce. The parties who thought they loved each other so much find they have only one thing in common—their unlucky offspring, who become bones of contention between warring parents. Couples who stay together end by having clandestine affairs that stir up a hornets' nest of injured feelings.

"Why not recognize the facts from the beginning? Provide for the secure emotional future of children and a rational living arrangement that allows adults the unfettered pursuit of their own designs?"

Rachel didn't answer. Unlike Marcus, she wasn't very experienced at arguments; she couldn't seem to put together a convincing retort. Yet, with all the conviction in her heart, she believed he was dead wrong.

"Besides," Marcus continued, "the death of the arranged marriage is a naive, uniquely American notion. In Europe weddings of convenience to consolidate wealth or power take place every day. And though they may be too romantic to admit it, I daresay quite a few of your countrymen post their bans for the very same reasons.''

To her consternation she had to concede the point. Though she'd believed in love when Des had courted her with flowers and candle-lit dinners, she'd discovered to her sorrow that political advantage, not reciprocal feelings, had figured most prominently in his plans. Even more sadly she'd come to the realization that her father's blessing had stemmed partly from the prospect of financial gain, though doubtless he'd convinced himself he was only thinking of her happiness.

"I can't believe you mean any of this," she responded, honesty forbidding an argument when she knew from experience just what he was talking about. "In a minute you're going to admit this is all a joke, and reveal your true purpose in asking me out tonight."

But Marcus wasn't joking.

"Problems like my need for an heir vis-à-vis my aversion to getting emotionally involved with someone require bold, sometimes unconventional solutions," he answered. "After thorough consideration, I've decided to take this step. By now it should come as no surprise that you're Alan's top candidate. And I must admit that, since meeting you, I concur. That's why, under the conditions I've outlined and pending further discussions to make certain we'd be compatible in raising a child, I'm asking you to marry me."

# Chapter Three

"I wouldn't dream of doing such a thing!" Rachel sprang to her feet, nearly upsetting her half-empty glass of sherry. "To think you'd propose marriage to me, one of your employees, based on third-party research!" she exclaimed. "And in the next breath, tell me it's to be merely a business arrangement! My God! We hadn't even *met* before today, and you expect to hire me as your child's mother, sow a baby in me as if I were...were...some kind of *field*!"

Unaccustomed to losing her temper, she cast about frantically for a better way to express herself, but the right words wouldn't come. I'll have to quit now, she thought, her mind racing. Even if that means I must go back to the States. I can't work for him after this.

"I'd appreciate it," she added severely, "if you'd call me a cab."

"Hold on half a moment." Coming around the table, Marcus caught her lightly by the wrist. "I fully understand your reaction," he whispered, standing so close the barman must have thought he was witnessing a lovers' quarrel. "In fact, I was expecting it. I know what I'm suggesting might seem outrageous at first blush—"

Rachel freed herself as inconspicuously as possible. "Try humiliating," she snapped. "I feel cheap, just being chosen as the object of your grand design!"

"Please don't." Clearly Marcus regretted having upset her. "I swear I didn't intend this as an insult," he said. "Quite the opposite. I have the highest respect for you, Rachel, or I wouldn't have made you the offer I did. You're the sort of woman one finds so rarely nowadays—decent, unassuming, loyal."

"In other words, a Girl Scout!"

He frowned, genuinely at a loss.

"Girl *Guide* to you."

The situation was almost funny; despite her anger Rachel suppressed a desire to laugh. She wondered whether the barman would phone for assistance if she took a swing at Marcus with her purse.

Her dark-haired escort did laugh, though guardedly. "All right," he conceded. "I deserved that. You're far more complex than my remark gives you credit for, as I've already come to realize. By portraying you as selfless, I was being less than candid. The truth is, I'm hoping to appeal to your self-interest.''

She was still vexed enough that his comment went against the grain. ''If you're referring to the money—'' she began heatedly.

''Beggin' yer pardon, gov'ner.'' With obvious reluctance, the barman approached. ''We got to close,'' he said. ''City regulations, yer know.''

''Yes, all right.'' Marcus turned back to her. ''Please,'' he asked. ''Walk with me along the river while I try to put things in better perspective. I won't keep you long.''

She couldn't say afterward why she agreed to accompany him. Perhaps it was because she'd promised to hear him out and she rarely broke a promise. Or maybe it was just plain curiosity, combined with the fact that he was still her boss. Deep down she was almost flattered now that she'd had time to cool down a bit. With his millions, he could afford to be choosy. And he wanted her.

Whatever her reasons, Rachel found herself keeping pace with Marcus a few minutes later as they cut across a public greensward below the stone water gate and turned onto the mist-wreathed promenade of Victoria Embankment.

''In a sense, I suppose, I was hoping you'd welcome my proposal,'' Marcus said, linking her arm through his as their footsteps echoed on the granite paving stones. ''When I read Alan's report, I was amazed, not just at how perfectly you suit my requirements but at the way my plan fits your life. You're not a man hater, but you've had it up to here, as they say, with marriage. After your experience with Ross, I don't blame you.

"Yet you love children and want one of your own. If you accept my offer, you can have it both ways. No emotional entanglements, no pain. Just a baby to hold in your arms. Plus the kind of financial security that will allow you to help others—like the children in your paintings."

He paused as if silently willing her to see things from his point of view. In response Rachel huddled deeper inside her raincoat. She had to admit that, unthinkable as it was, the scheme he'd outlined was tailored to her deepest desires. Against her will she found herself imagining how it might be to make love to this tall handsome stranger and later, to carry their child beneath her heart.

As for the waifs in her paintings, she'd wished more than once that she had the means to help them. If she had more money, perhaps she could contribute to the support of the day-care center for low-income families she'd visited several times near Spitalfields Market. She knew it was perennially short of funds.

Of course, that wasn't sufficient reason to marry someone. She wasn't that much of a Girl Scout.

In the distance, atop its crenellated tower beside the Houses of Parliament, Big Ben struck the hour.

Somewhere a foghorn boomed mournfully. Mingling with traffic sounds from the city, the notes spread like ripples in the air.

Turning away, Rachel stared at the dimly lit, fog-shrouded shape of the H.M.S. *Chrysanthemum*, which floated at anchor beside the river wall. Stubbornly the idea of becoming a mother took root.

"I forgot to add," said Marcus in a low voice, "that while one child would fulfill our contract, I wouldn't object to siring another at some future date. Though we're both 'only children,' as the saying goes, it's good to have siblings, don't you think?"

"Yes, I do," Rachel replied.

He didn't press her further, and they resumed their walk past Hungerford Footbridge and the Charing Cross ferry pier, not touching though they matched their strides effortlessly, as if they'd strolled that way together for years.

"I love the city at this hour best of all," Marcus observed as they halted again just outside the circle of light cast by one of the quay's ornate dolphin lamps. "My French mother abhorred the London damp and fog, but I fear they're part of my soul."

For some reason, the remark made Rachel focus on Marcus as a person. Here's a man, she acknowledged, who's lost his only son. Despite his life in the fast lane he's spent some desolate hours. He's been badly hurt, and he'll soon be forty. I can't blame him for wanting what I want.

Softly she addressed him. "It's getting late...."

He nodded, taking her hands so tentatively this time that she didn't pull away. "As it happens, I have to go to Paris tomorrow," he said. "I shall be gone for several days. I know you aren't disposed to accept my offer. But dare I ask you to consider it anyway while I'm gone? I've already excused you from work until Friday on special assignment."

On the verge of saying no, Rachel hesitated. She didn't like the high-handed way he'd arranged for her to take a leave of absence, any more than she cared for his proposed marital arrangement. A voice inside her had other ideas. It was urging her not to turn him down—yet. *Having a baby is important to you,* it reminded her. *So is seeing Marcus Davenport again.*

Of course the latter notion was ridiculous. Still she couldn't help feeling drawn to her tall dark employer—more drawn than she'd ever expected to feel toward a man again.

"I doubt it'll make any difference," Rachel said at last. "But I suppose I could think things over."

"Thank you very much."

Even in that murky light, his pleasure was unmistakable. He was standing so close she could imagine the soft brush of his breath against her cheek. She wondered suddenly if he might kiss her.

No sooner had the idea entered her head than he put his arms around her. "Since I've made you a bona fide proposal of marriage," he murmured, "perhaps I might be forgiven for kissing you good-night."

Caught against his unfamiliar bulk, with the aroma of his tobacco and a tangy, exotic aftershave filling her nostrils, Rachel didn't answer. A moment later his mouth descended on hers.

At first he pressed his advantage lightly, tasting her with deference as if she were some rare and expensive wine. Perhaps he feared the overture might frighten her away, cause her to change her mind. When she didn't pull back, his kiss deepened. Rapacious yet almost loving, his tongue parted her lips to probe moist and tender places.

For Rachel, it was as if the earth had tilted. She staggered a little in his arms. White-hot shafts of longing pierced her to the quick, igniting a need so compelling she'd never experienced anything like it— not even during the halcyon days of her courtship with Des. A primal emptiness raged at the center of her being, and it could be satisfied only by the most complete surrender.

Tears shone against her lashes as he drew back to look at her. She realized that though the experience had been a shattering one for her, he probably didn't have a similar reaction. Instead, he was just a man well versed in the art of making love, demonstrating his expertise as negligently as he drew breath. After his many conquests, she must be every bit as exciting as bread crusts for dessert.

She couldn't possibly know how affected Marcus really was. A master at hiding his softer emotions, he gave no hint except to crook one brow in homage.

"Here's Jervis now with the car," he said, casually taking her arm.

Marcus's feelings were anything but casual at the moment. He didn't want to fall in love again, yet here was a woman who might cause him to do just that. Her response to his kiss had nearly set him on his heels.

At the same time, he didn't want to hurt her. A charming mixture of passion and innocence, Rachel seemed almost untouched by her marriage. She had a delicacy about her, a sheltered quality he hadn't encountered before. Would it make him a cad if he were to risk the possibility she could fall in love with him?

With his brusque nature and the workaholic schedule of around-the-world meetings, he assured himself it wasn't likely any woman would feel that way over the long haul. He helped her back into the car, recalling that Deirdre had once said as much to his face. Just the same, Rachel posed enough of a threat to his peace of mind that Marcus was extremely thoughtful as they drove back to her Chelsea flat.

Politely but firmly she declined his offer to accompany her upstairs. They said good-night on the narrow stoop of Grace Tweedt's brick-and-stucco eighteenth-century residence. Rachel was certain the landlady was watching them from behind her curtains, and she purposely avoided looking in that direction.

To her everlasting gratitude, Marcus didn't attempt a second good-night kiss. The handshake he offered instead struck just the right note, lending credibility to Rachel's intended explanation of a business meeting with the boss if her landlady brought up the subject.

"Thank you for dinner," she said, struck by how much had happened in the short time since he'd first spoken those words. "Have a successful trip."

"I will."

For a moment they regarded each other in silence. "See you Friday," he added. "In my office, about one, if that's all right."

She nodded. "I'll have an answer for you then."

A sigh of relief escaped Rachel when she didn't encounter Mrs. Tweedt in either the elegant Georgian entry hall or on the first-floor landing. When she reached the sanctuary of her flat, she ran breathlessly to peer out the window. But Marcus was already gone. Only the Daimler's taillights, winking red as the car turned the corner onto Lawrence Street, gave evidence that she hadn't imagined the whole encounter.

Turning away, she leaned heavily against the wall. With her eyes shut tight, she relived his kiss, experiencing it again down to the very soles of her feet.

Her confused emotions were more than she could cope with. Sighing, she took off her coat and shoes and looked around her cramped apartment. Thanks to Marcus, she was seeing it in a new light. Done up in faded chintzes and well-worn mahogany, with a large measure of the available room taken up by her drawing table and a lumpy old-fashioned daybed, it was cheerful but hardly Rachel's idea of a real home.

On her income, of course, she was lucky to have it. Her Upper Cheyne Row address bespoke a convenient, even fashionable, part of the city. It would be a long time before she could afford anything more spacious in such a congenial neighborhood.

Rachel didn't mind that. What she did mind—and what she really saw when she surveyed her modest quarters—was years of lonely struggle to build her reputation as an artist while she turned a blind eye to amorous couples and longed to cuddle the children she painted.

Years in which she'd be free to remember Marcus Davenport's kiss.

Marrying him could change all that, she realized. Though he wouldn't care for her like the husband of her dreams, she'd have a real home that echoed with the laughter of children. She wouldn't find herself in a rocking chair someday, old and full of regret, with the ghosts of unborn children and grandchildren about her knees.

Of course there'd still be loneliness. Children, no matter how much one might love them, couldn't provide the total affection in a woman's life. And friends never really filled the gap. But no matter what Marcus envisioned, she wasn't the type to have an extramarital affair.

If she learned to care for him, hurt was a certainty. Already haunted by their embrace on the riverbank, she realized her heart might break if he continued to seek his pleasure in other women's arms.

Yet she'd been a neglected wife before and survived. She would have accepted that status willingly if Des had given her a child. Knowing what to expect from the outset in a relationship with Marcus might make it possible for them to coexist. If he was discreet, she'd be spared public embarrassment. They might even become friends after a fashion, entertaining during the holidays and attending their child's school programs together.

Changing to a flannel nightgown and old bathrobe, Rachel heated some cocoa on the gas ring and curled up in her most comfortable chair. I can't believe I'm giving his scheme the time of day, she thought, let alone serious consideration. It's diametrically opposed to every tenet I hold dear.

Yet the rocking-chair image persisted, and finally she went to her bookshelf for a dog-eared copy of *Seventeenth Century English Poets* she'd purchased recently at the Portobello Road Market. Flipping through its pages, she located the Andrew Marvell poem she'd been looking for.

"But at my back I always hear time's winged chariot hurrying near..." Marvell had written, inviting his readers to seize opportunity without hesitation.

Thoughtfully reading the rest of the poem, Rachel set the book aside. Maybe I should grab the brass ring Marcus is holding out to me, she thought, getting into bed and switching off the lamp. Life is short and I might not have the chance again. Might not have a chance to kiss Marcus Davenport again, you mean, her far-too-astute inner voice responded. It was a long time before she fell asleep.

For the next several days, Marcus and his unorthodox proposal were never very far from Rachel's mind. Relieved of the necessity to go into her office, she tried at first to work, only to consign each crumpled effort to the wastebasket. Finally she gave up altogether and went out to explore the city, despite occasional drizzle and a leaden sky.

Letting the spirit take her, Rachel wandered through contemporary art galleries in New Bond Street, fed the pigeons in wind-buffeted Trafalgar Square and prowled the quays of St. Katharine Docks with its crowded yacht basin near Tower Bridge.

She spent the better part of the next day at the Margaret Drew Bowes Center for Pre-school Children, which operated in a converted warehouse near Spitalfields Market. Already acquainted with its director, Jocelyn Banks, Rachel was allowed to help out with play supervision and assist the staff in serving a hot lunch. As she bandaged a bruised knee and dished up plates of what the British called "bangers and mash," Rachel gave careful individual attention to each clean but shabbily dressed youngster.

On Thursday, patches of blue sky reappeared. With Marcus's return looming nearer, Rachel struck out for suburban Richmond upon Thames via the District Underground. Though she'd heard a great deal about neighboring Syon Park, with its lovely Adam house and ornamental gardens that stretched along the riverbank, she was quite unprepared for its beauty.

The town of Richmond was both quaint and handsome, a treasure trove of tiny shops and eighteenth century terraces with names like Maids-of-Honour Row and the Wardrobe. During one of the office gossip sessions, Rachel had heard that Marcus owned a house in the neighborhood. To her, it seemed the kind of place where everyone knew everyone else's past firsthand from the beginning. It appeared to be a cozy, safe place to bring up children in an anonymous and sometimes threatening world.

She paid her last visit of the day to Kew Gardens, which was ablaze with yellow tulips. Finding a bench near the glass whale of Palm House conservatory, Rachel reluctantly addressed the business at hand.

There was a proposal of marriage on the table. It offered the chance to realize a lifelong dream, though it also violated some of her most cherished notions. She had promised the dashing tycoon who had made it to give him an answer the following afternoon.

Part of her—the conservative, old-fashioned part—urged flinging it back in his face. The primitive female in her counseled otherwise. So did her risk-taking self, a side of her nature just beginning to make itself known. This is your best chance to live life to the fullest, these contrary selves argued. Say you'd like to know him better before making up your mind.

Being scrupulously honest with herself, Rachel admitted she wanted to see Marcus again for his own sake. For someone who'd vowed to give up men, she was behaving rather strangely. But his tall frame and those enigmatic eyes, not to mention the scent and sound and feel of him, just wouldn't stay out of her thoughts.

You could be getting yourself into a whole lot of trouble, Rachel cautioned herself some time later as she boarded the tube back to London. Yet she was overcome by a sense of fatalism as she took her seat. For the present, she wouldn't turn down Marcus's proposal even though she wouldn't quite accept it, either. Instead, she'd ask that they spend more time together, comparing notes on child rearing and preferred living arrangements.

* * *

Marcus beamed when she gave him the news. If he'd had second thoughts since kissing her good-night on the riverbank, he'd apparently resolved them.

"Naturally I didn't expect a firm answer at once," he confided, striding around his desk to grasp her lightly by the shoulders. "I'm delighted you'll give my idea a chance. And I agree, we need to spend considerable time in each other's company before making any permanent commitment. This weekend presents the perfect opportunity. I've been asked to a house party near Minster Lovell, in Oxfordshire. You shall come with me. We'll leave tonight."

Taken aback, she considered his invitation. He was a powerful man, used to getting his way. It would be all too easy to let him take control. "I'm not sure your friends would appreciate a last-minute guest," she said.

"Nonsense, of course they would. If you like, I can phone them."

Rachel shrugged. She was imagining the sort of house Marcus's friends probably owned, with a park and a half dozen chimneys. No doubt there'd be a stable full of horses, a Rolls-Royce or two in the driveway. "I hate to sound like a spoilsport," she told him at last. "But I literally have nothing to wear for that kind of occasion."

Her admission drew a blank look before his eyes lit up with an idea. "Not to worry," he assured her, energetically pressing a button on his desk console.

As if she were some kind of genie, Mrs. Billingsham appeared.

"Rachel Vanden Ross, meet Enid Billingsham," Marcus said. "Enid, I'd like you to go shopping with Rachel this afternoon. She needs a few things for a weekend in the country. And, as a recent arrival in London, she hasn't had time to familiarize herself with the best shops."

If she thought the request odd, Enid Billingsham gave no sign. "Of course, sir," she answered, casting a quick speculative glance at Rachel. "I'll just get Miss Blakeney to answer your calls."

"Thanks." He turned to Rachel. "Nothing but the best and don't spare the horses," he said. "Make sure you charge everything to my account."

"Now see here—" Rachel's tone was adamant, causing the secretary to bite her lip "—I really can't accept such largesse." She spoke firmly, as if that put an end to the matter.

Marcus shook his head. "Of course you can. I can well afford it. Besides, if things don't work out, you can post the whole lot back to me special delivery. All right?"

Against her will, it occurred to Rachel that she owed him a modicum of cooperation if she was serious about considering his proposal. "I'm afraid I wouldn't even know what to buy," she hedged.

Marcus made an amused little shrug. "Well," he countered, "that's hardly fatal. Enid can advise you, if it comes to that. As for this weekend, I expect we shall be doing some riding. And dressing for dinner, of course."

For Rachel, who had accompanied her father and late husband on their travels but purchased most of her outfits back home in North Carolina, a London shopping adventure would be like flying blind. She was grateful the secretary would accompany her, even though she had her own very decided taste. Still she didn't answer him for a moment.

"You will do this for me, won't you, Rachel?" Marcus asked.

He was used to getting his way and, if they were to marry, she wouldn't want him to think that would always be the case. But whatever she decided about his proposal, a weekend with him in the country was just too tempting to miss.

"All right," she conceded, the beginnings of a smile dancing about the corners of her mouth. "Even though it's against my better judgment."

What followed was an afternoon Rachel would never forget. With the sleek secretary as her guide and chauffeured by Marcus's regular driver in the Daimler, she was introduced to the world of London fashion at its best.

They began at Harrods, where a liveried doorman helped them alight in front of the famous gray-and-gold awning with as much courtesy as if they were royalty. Unfamiliar with the huge upper-crust emporium, Rachel stared at its soaring brilliantly lit arcade and glittering aisles of merchandise.

"I propose we start with basics, if that's all right with you, Mrs. Vanden Ross," the secretary suggested in her low, cultivated voice as she guided Rachel to the lingerie department.

The bewildering selection of whisper-soft lacy underthings and nightclothes nearly proved to be Rachel's undoing. Unaccustomed to such luxury, she found it difficult to choose. After a lengthy session in one of the plush changing rooms, she decided on three changes of lingerie, a peach silk and lace nightgown with matching peignoir, and a pair of ivory satin pajamas that would have done Jean Harlow proud.

Next they purchased gloves, a breathtakingly expensive leather purse and sheer-as-gossamer stockings. The choice of a lovely midnight-blue wool suit, matching pumps and white pleated blouse took longer, as did a fitting for riding boots in gleaming calfskin.

"You *do* ride, I hope?" Enid Billingsham asked quietly as they headed for the tweeds in search of a riding jacket.

"Actually, yes." Gratefully Rachel recalled the sporadic lessons she'd received at her father's North Carolina farm.

"English or Western?"

"Both."

The woman nodded. "That's good," she answered. "As you might guess, it's all English here."

From Harrod's they traveled to Beauchamp Place and the Bruce Oldfield designer salon where, with Enid Billingsham's encouragement, Rachel selected a pair of dinner dresses totaling just under £2,000. One, a floor-length copper silk with a plunging front brought out russet highlights in her dark tresses she hadn't known she possessed. But her favorite was the knee-length black jersey with a boat neckline, a deep V in the back, long sleeves and double-ruffled hem. It made her feel glamorous and special, like Audrey Hepburn in *Roman Holiday*.

Next they visited a Sloane Street jeweler where the secretary convinced her Marcus would be extremely disappointed if she didn't choose a lustrous mid-length string of pearls.

Subsequent forays included brief stops at a specialty boutique for a riding hat, crop and beautifully tailored trousers, and a shop next-door to Prince Charles's shirtmaker for several exquisitely made ladies' shirts, a tan turtleneck and a winter-white cashmere pullover with matching slacks. The pullover was embroidered with tiny pearls about the neck and shoulders.

Next came a whirlwind visit to a beauty salon, where the pink-coated attendant talked Rachel into allowing her hair to be sheared to a fluffy length that just skimmed her shoulders. The woman also applied glossy nail polish and makeup with a practiced hand.

I hardly recognize myself, Rachel thought, noting the secretary's undisguised admiration. She couldn't deny that the new hairdo plus blue-violet eye shadow, velvety black mascara and moist crushed-berry lip gloss had transformed her into a beauty.

Certain they'd finished their shopping spree, Rachel was a bit surprised when Marcus's secretary suggested they return to Sloane Street so Rachel could choose more shoes at Bruno Magli and some additional woolens at Gordon Lowes. Ordinarily, spending so much money on herself would have made her feel guilty. But Marcus had asked her to do it for him, and she'd agreed to cooperate. It wouldn't do, she decided, shaking her head over the stack of boxes in the Daimler's front seat, to think about the cost.

She balked a minute later when they halted before a small exclusive furrier's with striped awnings above its mullioned glass windows. "This is *definitely* too much," she proclaimed to Enid Billingsham in no uncertain terms. "I have no intention of charging a fur coat to Mr. Davenport's account!"

Without a doubt, the secretary guessed her previous claims that Marcus "expected it" wouldn't work this time. "All the women who attend the Nevilles' party will be wearing furs," she began, trying a different tack.

Stubbornly Rachel rejected the notion. "I understand you're only trying to help me," she said. "It's part of your job. But I wouldn't feel right about something like this."

Enid Billingsham shrugged. She hadn't risen to her position at Elite through any lack of diplomacy. But she would feel remiss in her duty if she let Rachel go down to Oxfordshire in that terribly middle-class raincoat.

"Well, wouldn't it be fun just to go inside and try on a few jackets?" she proposed. "It's still early, and I don't have to go back to the office this afternoon. We don't have to buy anything."

Rachel gave her a startled look. Throughout their shopping expedition, the secretary hadn't so much as fingered a silk scarf. "Do you mean you'd try on some of the jackets, too?" she asked.

"Well, of course!" the woman answered readily. "It isn't often I get the chance."

Studying her, Rachel considered. She had to admit Enid Billingsham had been polite, friendly and unfailingly helpful. It was hardly fair to deny her a little fun.

"All right," she conceded. "I guess we have the time."

Inside the fur salon, the secretary coaxed Rachel into putting on her new black party dress and spike heels before trying on any of the jackets.

Slipping on several furs over her own gray business suit, Mrs. Billingsham modeled them with obvious pleasure before excusing herself to make a phone call. She didn't return to the fitting salon for a few minutes. Stunned by her new image and lost in imagining what Marcus would say if he could see her, Rachel continued to pirouette before the three-way mirror in a glamorous succession of minks, foxes and sables.

"Well, sir? What do you think?"

The words were Enid Billingsham's, and Rachel—swathed in that moment in richly glowing Russian sable—turned around to answer them. With a quickening heartbeat, she found herself pinned beneath Marcus's deep blue gaze.

# Chapter Four

For a moment no one spoke. Tension in the room spun out fine and fragile as a crystal goblet. Rachel had the feeling that one word—the *wrong* word—could shatter it into a million fragments.

Clearly Marcus was startled at her transformation. Slowly, deliberately, as if he had an eternity for the task, he raked his gaze from the tips of her suede pumps past slender ankles and shapely calves to the delicate line of her chin as it nestled against glistening sable. Motionless as a doe caught in a hunter's sights, Rachel looked back at him half in profile. There was something vulnerable yet infinitely alluring about the wing of dark hair that curved against her cheek's high color. He wanted to lift it aside with one finger and replace it with a kiss.

Beautiful, he thought in amazement, meeting the flood of uncertainty in her eyes. How could I have failed to see it earlier? She's easily one of the most beautiful women I've ever met.

He wasn't sure how this discovery might affect his peace of mind. With a little shake of his head, he crossed the space between them. She caught her breath as his fingers sank into lush yielding fur to fasten on her shoulders.

"Well," he said in the offhand, faintly ironic way she was beginning to recognize. "I see our jaunt into the country will be more provocative than I expected."

The secretary's presence forgotten, Rachel let her hands rest against the roughly textured tweed of his jacket. She was burningly aware of the hard male physique beneath it. "I want you to know we were just trying these on for fun."

Marcus cut her off with typical decisiveness. "You shall have one, of course. The little number you're wearing, if it meets with your approval. I know it does with mine."

He was looking at her as if she were something good to eat and he was "slimming," as the British called dieting. She had the distinct feeling he liked what he saw but was somehow displeased by his own reaction.

She wasn't quite sure how to answer him. Her moment's hesitation sealed the jacket's fate. Instructing a clerk to charge it to his account, Marcus turned his attention back to her.

"I have a hunch you'll be glad of its warmth this afternoon," he added, as if to lay any further objections to rest by an appeal to practicality. "The weather's taken a definite turn for the raw, I'm afraid. And there's no damp like England's. By the way, since we're leaving directly for Oxfordshire, you might want to substitute something more casual for that extremely charming dress."

Rachel continued to stare at him. If they were leaving on their weekend trip directly from the furrier's salon, what was she supposed to do about luggage? Use the odd collection of boxes and totes she'd acquired on her shopping trip?

"I don't see how we can do that," she argued. "I haven't had time to pack."

Marcus lowered his arms to encircle her waist. "I took the liberty of asking Gucci to send around some luggage," he said, smiling down at her. "Enid and my man Jervis can pack for you while you change."

When he looked at her like that, with a warmth that seemed far more personal than businesslike, she wanted to melt like a snowdrift in April. Yet conversely Marcus brought out her stubborn streak.

She didn't budge. "I'm still going to need a toothbrush," she said.

The subtle fragrance she wore, with its grace notes of lily of the valley, was invading his senses. With genuine reluctance he dropped his hands.

"Pan Neville stocks every conceivable necessity for her guests," he answered. "You'll be well provided for."

Leaving the fur salon without a chance to collect a few personal belongings, Rachel knew, would throw her even more off balance. She'd feel her destiny had been taken out of her hands.

Things were moving too fast. She'd been in England three months, known Marcus Davenport only a few days. There had *been* no weekend trip on the agenda when she'd left her flat around noon to meet him at his office.

Where's your spirit of adventure? she prodded herself. You know this is something you want to do. "All right," she conceded. "Give me half a minute to change."

Ducking back into the fitting room, Rachel slipped out of the black party dress and handed it out the door. In its place she donned her new ivory sweater and slacks. Quickly she softened the lines of her new coiffure with a few strokes of her hairbrush.

Then, pausing for a moment with her fingers still curled around the brush handle, she stared at her reflection. Was the slightly astonished-looking young woman about to run off for the weekend with Marcus Davenport really Luther Vanden's sheltered and very proper daughter? What had become of the modest self-effacing wife who'd accompanied Desmond Ross from one North Carolina whistle-stop to another in her serviceable cloth coat?

Even the new stand-alone Rachel who'd come to London and established life on her own terms seemed displaced by the exotic creature looking back at her. Meeting Marcus has turned my life inside out, she thought. I feel as if I'm stepping off a cliff without knowing if there will be anyone there to catch me.

Her new Gucci cases were neatly stacked in the shop's foyer when she emerged. Standing beside them, Rachel felt like the heroine of a children's story, plucked from a drab existence by a beneficent stranger.

Well, that's hardly the case, she thought, shrugging on her new jacket with a thrill of pleasure despite her reservations. Her independent risk-taking self was alive and kicking, thank you. Who else would have dared consider Marcus's proposal, if not that Rachel? Who else could she trust now to help her make up her mind?

The charge slip for her jacket was signed, and Marcus thanked his secretary and sent her home in the Daimler.

"What about us?" Rachel asked when Jervis and Enid Billingsham had gone.

"I've brought the Jaguar," he answered, drawing on supple black leather gloves. "I'll be driving us down myself."

Deftly Marcus stowed her cases in the trunk of his sleek gray automobile. After settling Rachel in the luxurious passenger seat, he got behind the wheel and turned his key in the ignition. The deep-throated engine growled to life.

"Now then, Rachel Ross," he said, giving her a speculative look as they darted into the stream of late-afternoon traffic. "We're off to an adventure of unknown proportions, one that could change both our lives."

To say Marcus was a skillful driver would have been an understatement. Quick and confident behind the wheel, he seemed to enjoy doing battle with the mob of buses, trucks and cars that clogged the city's main arteries.

Rachel was all but oblivious to the passing scene. To her, the congested thoroughfares and seemingly endless frieze of stone buildings and crowds of pedestrians funneling into the tube stations were little more than a blur. Her attention was trained on Marcus as he maneuvered the car expertly through the heavy traffic.

If we were lovers, I might rest a hand on his knee, she thought. He might respond by giving me a little squeeze.

As it was, they were still relative strangers. They'd barely even spoken since leaving the furrier's shop. As they entered the westbound motorway and picked up speed, Marcus appeared to concentrate solely on his driving. He seemed actually to revel in the traffic's hectic pace, perhaps as an antidote to the mental stress of the workweek he'd just put behind him.

Despite his obvious sophistication with women, Rachel decided it was possible he didn't know what to say to her. Their situation was hardly ordinary. Yet they'd have to converse if they were to get to know each other. She couldn't see how that would be any easier amid a throng of weekend guests.

After they passed the spires and turrets of Oxford, Marcus switched to more leisurely country roads. As if he suddenly remembered her presence, he began to engage her in conversation.

"I realize it may be something of a tall order," he acknowledged with a boyish grin. "But, if you wouldn't mind, I'd like to hear about your philosophy of raising children."

Haltingly at first, because his question focused on the somewhat sensitive raison d'être of their relationship, Rachel tried to put her feelings into words. Gradually she warmed to her subject, her cheeks glowing with animation as she explained that she considered unconditional love the best tonic—expressed frequently with hugs, milk and cookies and a genuine interest in the most trivial details of a child's daily existence.

"Of course it's important to instill values," she told him. "Set standards and teach youngsters to aim high. Let them know there will be unpleasant consequences if they overstep their boundaries. But, in my opinion, love's the basic thing. That and being there when they need you. They should be able to feel there's always someone they can count on. Someone who believes in them and thinks they're truly special. A safe haven from which they can venture forth to try their mettle against the world."

She fell silent as the Jaguar's tires bit into the pavement of a low stone bridge. Beneath it, a brook tumbled over its rock-strewn bed.

"I couldn't agree with you more," Marcus replied after a moment. "That's what I lacked as a boy, you know. The sense of loving arms to run to. Plus the feeling that it mattered to someone if I was chosen for the rugby team or won a spelling match."

Unwilling to interrupt what she suspected was an unaccustomed confidence, Rachel waited.

"My parents died when I was quite young," he added, throwing her an enigmatic look. "I was raised by a great-aunt, whose tidy, circumscribed life was thoroughly disarranged by an active eight-year-old. She did her best, I know that. And in her own way even loved me, I suppose. She just didn't know how to show it. And it would have meant the earth."

"Where's your aunt now?" she asked, gently laying a hand on his arm. "Do you still see her sometimes?"

He shook his head. "She died the year I finished at Cambridge. In case you were wondering, she was my last living relative."

Just then they rounded a bend in the road. Through a break in the trees, Rachel glimpsed a red brick manor house. Set atop a rise backed by a thick copse of woods, it commanded a spectacular view.

"There's the Nevilles' place now," Marcus said casually. "We'll be arriving in a few moments."

The country seat of Pandora and Whitney Neville outstripped even Rachel's expectations. A classic example of Georgian design, the three-story mansion boasted a large central structure flanked by two matching wings. Broad stone steps swept upward to the first-floor main entrance, which was situated on the lower of two columned porches. Smoke curled from various chimneys.

She hadn't been far wrong when she'd imagined a Rolls-Royce or two in the driveway. She counted a Silver Shadow and a Bentley, the latter being handed over to one of the Nevilles' retainers. The car's male owner, his much younger blond companion and a slim brown-haired woman, shivering in cashmeres and tweeds, all turned toward Marcus in obvious delight.

Rachel's guess that the brown-haired woman was Pandora Neville proved accurate.

"I'm so delighted you could make it for once!" their hostess exclaimed, kissing him on the cheek. "And how delightful that you've brought a friend. Do let's get out of this damp before I catch my death!"

Leaving the servant to park the Jaguar in the garage, Rachel and Marcus mounted the steps in Pan Neville's wake. Her husband, Whit, a distinguished-looking man in his early fifties, and several other guests were waiting in the black-and-white marble foyer.

For Rachel, entering the Neville mansion was like stepping into another world. I suppose I knew people lived this way, she thought, catching a glimpse of herself in an eight-foot mirror. I just never expected to be a part of it.

During the introductions, she had the strong feeling she was accepted simply because she was with Marcus. Yet the tightly knit group's curiosity was an almost tangible thing, particularly after he let slip the fact that she was Luther Vanden's daughter.

"I do believe you're the first person I've ever met who's connected to an American evangelist," remarked the cool blonde from the Bentley, whom Pan had introduced as Cynthia Aston-Jones. "I'm dying to hear all about your experiences."

Rachel recoiled slightly despite her best intentions. "There's really very little to tell," she answered in a low voice.

Mercifully Pan Neville was an alert and considerate hostess. "Cynthia, dear!" she chirped with a reproving little shake of her head. "If we must quiz Rachel, please let's do so in front of the fire. I'm sure we're all dying for a drink."

Once inside the surprisingly cozy and cheerful drawing room with its casual arrangements of hothouse flowers, brightly blazing hearth and comfortable overstuffed furniture, their hostess introduced an array of conversational gambits. With the focus shifted away from her, Rachel was free to sip her mulled wine and study her surroundings. Since much of the talk centered around social events and the latest theater offerings in London, she had very little to contribute.

Dinner in the formal dining room, off an East Indian service that had been in the Neville family for several generations, was a full-dress affair watched over by a collection of ancestral portraits. Warned by Marcus what to expect, Rachel chose her low-cut copper silk. She was rewarded with a definite gleam of physical interest when he knocked at her door to escort her downstairs. She could feel the heat of his gaze as he lowered it to trace the white curve of her bosom, then raised it again to meet her eyes.

As they were descending one side of the mansion's curving symmetrical staircase, he asked if she'd mind playing an affectionate role with him. "It might help pave the way for a future marriage announcement," he explained with a rakish grin. "I hope you won't find it too difficult."

Wondering how thoroughly he intended to play his part, Rachel promised to do her best.

During the five-course meal and afterward when they returned to the drawing room for brandy and amateur theatricals, Marcus was as attentive as any woman could wish. Several times she caught Cynthia Aston-Jones watching them with a puzzled expression. It was obvious the angular, haughty blonde considered Rachel an unlikely choice for Marcus.

It wouldn't surprise me if she has a "thing" for him, Rachel decided. I can see how any woman would, but that doesn't mean it's reciprocated.

If she'd been asked in advance, Rachel would have guessed Marcus was something of a night owl. To her amazement, as the theatricals disbanded in favor of desultory conversation, he stifled a yawn and murmured something about turning in. "To be honest," he remarked to no one in particular, "it's been an exhausting week."

Not about to be left behind in the company of strangers, Rachel promptly added that she was tired, as well. Innocent of the impression she created, she linked her arm with his and accompanied him upstairs.

"Well done," Marcus applauded as they reached the south bedroom wing. "As I'm sure you realize, we've been provided with adjoining rooms. The rumor mill downstairs will have us cozily ensconced in bed together."

They had halted outside her door, and Rachel raised her face to his in astonishment.

He was standing very close. "That's not such a terrible idea, is it?" he whispered, lowering his mouth to hers.

I wouldn't want them to think it, she was about to answer. Kissing her with the same controlled passion that had so disarmed her on the riverbank, Marcus drove every rational thought from her mind. Beneath her copper silk bodice, her nipples hardened into telltale nuggets as he crushed her against his chest. Rachel found herself overwhelmed with a longing she'd felt only once before—the first time he'd taken her in his arms.

Deaf to the conversation drifting from the drawing room, and blind to every reality but Marcus, Rachel parted her lips. The gesture encouraged him. Tightening his embrace, he ravaged her mouth, taking complete possession of it in a rapacious yet deeply tender kiss.

I want him more than life, more than anything, Rachel realized, her heart hammering beneath her breasts. I, who didn't plan on getting involved with a man again. I can't believe this is happening.

Keenly aware of her reaction and his own body's swift response to it, Marcus drew back to search her face. A moment later he released her. "Sleep well, Rachel," he said, sending her crashing without a hint of what it cost him. "I wish you pleasant dreams."

# Chapter Five

Morning came and with it the promise of clement weather. Sunlight and even a glimmer of warmth filtered through rose-sprigged curtains as Rachel smoothed her hair into a tidy equestrian's knot. She had to admit her new riding clothes presented quite a contrast to the faded jeans and bulky sweaters she usually wore at home.

Wandering downstairs, she found Pan Neville and several guests, including Marcus, already seated in the sunny breakfast room. Cynthia Aston-Jones was not among them; apparently she'd chosen to sleep in.

Responding to a chorus of friendly greetings, Rachel expressed the hope that she hadn't kept anyone waiting.

"Nonsense, my dear, we're taking our time as usual," Pan assured her with a ready smile. "Margaret has just replenished the buffet. Please help yourself."

Selecting fresh fruit, a coddled egg and several rashers of bacon from the covered silver dishes of Pan's Sheraton sideboard, Rachel slipped into her seat with Marcus's courteous assistance.

She couldn't help noticing how handsome he looked in his snowy-white shirt, tan trousers and black riding boots. A tweed jacket with a black chesterfield collar was slung casually over the back of his chair.

Grateful for the piping-hot American-style coffee poured for her by a crisply uniformed maid, Rachel tried not to think about the previous night's encounter. But it had left a lasting impression, and as Marcus passed her the sugar, she imagined she could read similar sentiments in his eyes.

He claimed her hand some minutes later as they were walking to the stables. "Sleep well?" he inquired, forcing her to look up at him.

"Actually I was a bit restless," she confessed, then blushed at what she seemed to be admitting.

"So was I," he answered. "I don't understand it. The Nevilles' guest rooms are famous for the comfort of their feather beds."

Two of the other guests, Max and Georgia Weathers, caught up with them as they entered the stable yard. A groom had brought out several horses for their inspection.

"Come on," said Marcus, leaving off his teasing. "Let's have a closer look."

Rachel could see that the Nevilles' thoroughbreds were among the finest; there wasn't a loser in the lot. Still she couldn't suppress a twinge of disappointment when the groom suggested a docile-looking bay instead of the spirited chestnut filly that had caught her eye.

Guessing at her emotions, Marcus took hold of the filly's reins. "What about this sprightly miss?" he asked. "Think you can handle her?"

Rachel beamed, captivated that he'd taken the trouble to discern her wishes. "I'd certainly like to try," she said. "She reminds me of a horse I rode at home."

Pleased with her enthusiasm, Marcus helped her into the saddle. Moments later he was astride his own selection, one of their hosts' prize stallions. The huge animal reared slightly as they clattered out of the stable yard.

Pan Neville and Max Weathers took the lead as they cantered across the park beneath the trees. Rachel and Marcus followed, with Georgia Weathers and another guest, David Llewellyn, bringing up the rear.

The day was fresh and fair, without even a hint of rain. Though the trees were still leafless, Rachel could see they were about to bud. Already a few fragile wildflowers were poking up through damp, decaying leaves.

Sitting erect and holding the reins loosely but firmly, Rachel exchanged a look of pure delight with Marcus as they splashed across a stony creek bed. Water scattered in shimmering droplets. Moments later they were crossing into rougher terrain, a wood choked with vines on either side of the path, some of them hung with blood-red berries. The mingled scents of leather and moist rich earth filled her nostrils.

Oh, she thought, caught up in the exhilaration of the moment. Just to be alive and riding out in the English countryside with Marcus beside me. It's like a dream.

"Can you jump?" he shouted a few minutes later, pointing at a five-barred gate that separated the little wood from an open field.

"Of course!"

Rachel's answer rang out with far more certainty than she felt. She had jumped several times on her father's farm but never in an English saddle. It was going to be interesting, to say the least.

David Llewellyn caught up with them just as they sailed across. "Well done!" he exclaimed as Marcus threw her an approving look. "Who says the Yanks aren't good with horses?"

Crossing several more fields and thickets on the Nevilles' property, they emerged on a country road that appeared to follow the banks of a fair-sized stream. Clear as glass, it flowed between waving plumes of waterweed. Birds sang in the filtered light.

"That's the Windrush, one of our most beautiful rivers," Marcus told her as they slowed their horses to a walk. "It joins the Thames near the Berkshire border."

Several miles down the road, they approached an arched stone bridge. Beside it, a hip-roofed cottage was half-hidden among the trees.

"What a charming spot!" Rachel exclaimed. "Do you suppose we'll be asked in for tea and crumpets? Or strawberries and clotted cream?"

Marcus laughed, aware she was gently poking fun at the typical repasts in British novels. "Hungry already?" he teased. "It must be the country air."

He went on to explain that the dwelling they were approaching was called Bridge Cottage. "In former times," he said, "a bridge tender lived there. His job was to exact a toll from Welsh shepherds who drove their flocks this way to market in the east of England. The bridge was designed so that it narrows to a single lane, thus making it easier for the tender to count the sheep."

Across the river, the gray-brown Burford stone cottages of Minster Lovell greeted them. Flanked by squared-off chimneys, they huddled under thatched or stone roofs along the village's single thoroughfare. Most were so covered with creepers and lichen they seemed constructed of the earth itself.

Yet the place was anything but somber. Early spring flowers brightened a garden by the millrace. The homey smell of baking bread assailed the riding party. Several residents waved a friendly greeting as the group passed.

Marcus explained that newly renovated Old Swan Hotel had been standing the better part of five centuries. "Those Welsh drovers I told you about used to stop there," he said. "So did Richard III. Unlike them, he probably didn't have to share a room."

Beyond a cricket field at the edge of the village, the road rose to meet the higher elevation of Minster Lovell Hall. It stood starkly against a blue sky, and the crumbling remains of its ruined tower seemed to brood about long-past days. Swallows dipped through windowless arches that had been laid in the fifteenth century. From some hidden cranny came the mournful cooing of a dove.

"What do you say we dismount and have a look 'round?" Pan Neville suggested. "Some of us are familiar with the place, of course. But I doubt if Rachel has seen it."

Everyone seemed pleased with the suggestion and turned their horses loose in a green, grassy courtyard.

For a while they walked about the site, enjoying the fresh air as Pan pointed out the hall's significant architectural details.

"I'm afraid that's the extent of my services as a guide," their hostess laughed after a bit, brushing several burrs from her trousers. "Marcus knows the history of Minster Lovell Hall much better than I do. Those who haven't heard it yet may want to stay awhile and persuade him to tell it. I hope he'll forgive me if I settle for a hot cup of tea at the Swan instead."

As if by unspoken agreement, the Weatherses and David Llewellyn opted for a visit to the village tearoom. They rode off, leaving her with Marcus.

Noting that he seemed satisfied with the arrangement, Rachel made herself comfortable on a warm stone. Neither of them said anything for a moment, and she wondered if he'd set things up so they could be alone.

His dark hair ruffled in the breeze as Marcus cupped his hands and lit a cigarette. He appeared more relaxed than she'd ever seen him before, and he stretched out on the grass at her feet.

"As Pan mentioned earlier," he said, "the hall was built in 1440 by William Lovell. William was a powerful man, in good graces with the crown. Unfortunately, his grandson Francis lacked his political craftiness. He backed the wrong side in the War of the Roses and was declared a traitor. Henry VII confiscated his estates.

"Later Francis was reported killed at the Battle of Stoke. Legend has it he survived and went into hiding here, known only to a faithful servant. When the servant died suddenly, Francis was trapped in a room that opened only from the outside. He supposedly starved to death.''

Rachel made a face. ''What a terrible end that must have been! I hope it's just a story.''

He shrugged. ''Some say it's more than that. Several centuries after his disappearance, workmen found the complete skeleton of a man in a hidden chamber.''

The tale of Francis Lovell wasn't the ruin's only legend, Rachel learned. Marcus went on to recount a far more ancient one, revolving about nearby St. Kenelm's Church.

''Kenelm was the seven-year-old son of a Mercian king,'' he said. ''He was murdered by his wicked sister. A dove supposedly flew off to tell the Pope, who ordered an investigation of the boy's death. Meanwhile, the sister was struck blind in retribution.''

Looking at her, Marcus felt as if a completely separate conversation, one that didn't depend on words, had been weaving itself through the fabric of his storytelling. *I wonder if she knows how lovely she is,* he thought. *Or how much I'm beginning to want her.*

For her part, Rachel couldn't help thinking what a handsome man he was. Lean and long limbed, he had an athlete's figure, with broad powerful shoulders and a trim waist. She wanted to smooth back the thick hair that fell over his forehead. His eyes seemed able to gaze into her very soul.

Rachel wasn't usually given to lustful daydreaming, but she found herself imagining what it would be like to make love to Marcus. How would it feel, she wondered, to lie tangled up with him between breeze-scented sheets? To know I was going to have his baby?

His growing hold on her wasn't just physical, any more than it arose exclusively from desire to be a mother. As she got to know Marcus, with his dark moods and his penchant for teasing, the protective urges and generosity that balanced his lone-wolf nature had made liking part of the equation. It would be difficult, she admitted, not to see him again.

She was startled when he reached for her hand. Slender and ringless, adorned only by the pink polish she'd acquired in the London beauty salon, it lay imprisoned in his stronger, browner grasp.

"Wouldn't you say that, despite its melancholy history, Minster Lovell Hall's a better setting for a marriage proposal than Gordon's?" he asked her after a moment.

She could detect no hint of teasing in his dark blue eyes.

"Yes, I suppose it is," she answered, wondering what would follow.

"Then perhaps I'd better ask you again."

He didn't actually go that far. Giving her hand a squeeze, he let it go and changed the subject. Soon afterward, he suggested they should be getting back and offered to help her remount.

Though the brief moments when he'd held her hand and assisted her into the saddle were their only physical contact during the outing, Rachel felt extraordinarily close to him as they returned to the Neville estate.

I'm falling in love with him, she thought in amazement as he smiled brilliantly at her and quickened their pace. Just a touch of his hand and I melt like warm taffy. Though they hardly knew each other, she wanted nothing more than to be with him. She'd be content to spend the rest of her life in his strong and loving arms.

Once they returned to the other guests, she and Marcus lounged about. They rested up for the evening's entertainment, a private concert by Cynthia Aston-Jones, whom Rachel learned performed regularly as a singer on the London stage. Henry Cavendish, the rangy blonde's much-older companion, turned out to be one of her wealthy backers.

Dressed for the evening in her black party dress and pearls, Rachel earned several appreciative looks, including one from David Llewellyn. Not to be outdone by the other man's admiration, Marcus whispered an extravagant compliment in her ear as they took their places at the table.

Struggling with her new-found feelings for Marcus, Rachel found it difficult to pay attention during Cynthia's performance. Something about the way the blond singer looked at Marcus made her wonder if they'd been intimate in the past. The woman certainly appeared to be carrying a torch for him.

I won't think about that, Rachel told herself in no uncertain terms, giving the genuinely talented Miss Aston-Jones a warm smile, and applauding when she'd finished. I have a future with Marcus if I want it. Maybe I even have the chance to ease his hurt and teach him to love again.

When they went up to bed later that evening, Marcus stepped inside her room without being asked. "You might be interested to know, there's been gossip about our sleeping in separate rooms," he said, resting one hand against the curve of bare back exposed by her black cocktail dress. "Perhaps we should make this look good. What would you say to my staying with you here?"

"I don't understand." Taken aback, Rachel retreated from him a little. Was this his usual mode of operation, she wondered, when staying at the Nevilles' with a female guest?

Neither of them had switched on a lamp. Curtains billowed in the breeze as she strained to see his face in the faint moonlight that filtered through the open windows.

"I'm not the sort to sleep with a man who isn't my husband," she told him. No matter how much I might want to, she added silently.

Though she couldn't be certain, she thought she saw a reaction in his eyes.

"Naturally," he said, letting go of her. "As far as intimacy between us is concerned, I'll respect your feelings. But it mightn't be a bad idea for us to try sleeping together. We ought to find out if I snore and you pinch the bed covers."

The suggestion was outrageous and Rachel was on the verge of protest. She didn't care whether or not the Nevilles and their guests thought she was a prude for not sleeping with Marcus.

On the other hand she realized their gossip meant something to him. Perhaps his masculine pride was wounded. Maybe he didn't want outsiders to guess at the utilitarian nature of their relationship. Reluctantly she conceded it wouldn't make much difference if he spent the night.

"I suppose it would be all right, under the circumstances you're describing," she said, switching on the light.

"Good," he answered, keeping his voice expressionless. "I'll just go get my things."

The moment he left, Rachel barricaded herself in the bathroom to change into her white satin pajamas. Though their lush fabric clung to every curve, they were far less revealing than her only other choice, the semitransparent peach nightgown and negligee.

When Marcus returned clad in a foulard silk pajama bottom, she was seated demurely at the old-fashioned dressing table, brushing her hair. She couldn't help but gaze at his bare chest, with its inverted triangle of coarse dark hair that tapered off toward his waistband.

"These are in your honor," he remarked, indicating his pajama trousers. "I usually sleep in the nude."

Rachel flushed but didn't answer. He got in bed ahead of her, stretching out on the side she was accustomed to using and leaving her to turn out the light. She felt terribly awkward, pulling back the bed covers and getting in beside him.

"Good night," he said after a moment, his deep voice so close to her ear that she jumped a little. "I hope we both can get some rest."

Lying beside him in the big double bed was an unnerving experience. To Rachel's combined relief and chagrin, he fell asleep almost immediately, his soft even breathing destroying any notion she had that he might suffer from desire.

As her eyes adjusted to the darkness, she was able to see him more clearly. In sleep, the look of a hard-driving executive that he usually wore gave way to that of a vulnerable, very human man. One whom, as she viewed the fringe of dark lashes that lay against his cheek, she could easily imagine as a boy.

Remembering the emotional deprivation of his childhood and the loss of his son, not to mention the treachery of that son's mother, Rachel's heart went out to him. She couldn't imagine how Deirdre Davenport could have wanted anyone but him.

Please, she whispered to the powers greater than herself as she waited for sleep. If it's possible, let Marcus learn to love me back a little. Otherwise I think my heart will break.

Please, she whispered to the powers below. Help
Marcus to see tonight that his life's worth something
beyond his work. Give me just a little time with
him, for his sake and mine . . .

# Chapter Six

Rachel sat quietly in the Jaguar's passenger seat the
following afternoon as they returned to London.
Smoothing down the skirt of her blue wool suit, she
stole a glance at Marcus's firmly sculpted profile. As
usual it was impossible to guess what was on his
mind.

She couldn't believe that they'd spent the night
together. Several of their fellow guests had exchanged knowing looks over the breakfast table, but
nothing had happened between her and Marcus.
He'd been up, dressed and on his way downstairs
before she was out of bed.

It didn't surprise her that she'd slept a little late.
The luminous dial of the bedside clock had read
nearly half past two by the time she'd drifted off to

a fitful sleep. Lying beside Marcus, so close to him yet inexorably separate, hadn't been conducive to an untroubled mind.

Watching him now and remembering the strong sense of connectedness she'd felt between them at Minster Lovell Hall, Rachel wondered if she'd been imagining things. I hope not, she thought with a little shake of her head. Because just a glimpse of what we could have together...

Marcus turned to her as abruptly as if she'd spoken. "Maybe I'm premature in asking," he said in his deep, faintly rough voice. "But we've had a chance this weekend to get better acquainted. Have you given any more thought to my proposal?"

She didn't answer him for a moment, but there wasn't any use pretending—not even to herself. In her heart, she knew it was too late already to tell him no.

"Actually, I've decided to accept," she said, giving him a shy look.

"But that's wonderful!" The Jaguar swerved a little as he reached over to squeeze her hand. "I hope what I'm about to tell you won't make you change your mind."

Thrown slightly off balance, Rachel waited for him to elaborate.

"I have to go out of the country for two weeks," he explained, lighting a cigarette. "It's unfortunate, I know, just when I'd hoped we could spend some additional time together. But it can't be helped."

Blowing out a little cloud of smoke, he glanced at her for her reaction. If being with me is so important to him, she wondered, why doesn't he ask me to come along? But she realized that option probably hadn't occurred to him.

"Maybe it's for the best," he added when she didn't speak. "After this weekend, I'm sure you'll agree . . . our rather unorthodox courtship does have its awkward moments."

Sharing a bed but not making love had been his idea, not hers, but she didn't express her thoughts aloud. The impersonal tone of their conversation was making it difficult for her to believe they'd just agreed to marry.

"In the interest of propriety, not to mention the press of business," he went on, "I'd prefer a brief engagement. What would you say to tying the knot at a civil ceremony when I return?"

He matter-of-factly named a date.

Rachel was stunned that it was only two weeks hence but couldn't think of a valid reason to wait. After all, theirs was to be a marriage of convenience—at least on his part. He'd made that absolutely clear.

"I suppose I could be ready by then," she said.

Marcus pulled off the roadway at that and sealed their betrothal with a kiss.

He didn't call once during his two-week absence. Rachel wasn't even sure of his itinerary. Busy with more shopping, this time for her trousseau, she reasoned he was giving her time to get used to the idea of their marriage—and a chance to reconsider without pressure on his part.

On the afternoon she'd accepted his proposal, he'd suggested they honeymoon in Brittany. He owned a farm there, situated in the Bigouden area of the Cornouaille coast. It was the *environnement* of his mother's childhood.

He'd gone on to warn her that the whitewashed stone cottage there was primitive and isolated, though it had the advantage of being near an unspoiled beach. If the atmosphere proved too quiet for her, they could always drive to Pointe du Raz or ride into one of the local villages. He knew a neighbor who could provide them with horses.

Surprised and delighted that he would suggest such a romantic setting, Rachel had quickly given her approval. She had a hunch mystical Brittany would go a long way toward explaining her soon-to-be husband's moody Celtic streak.

Thanks to her new familiarity with London shops, she was able to make the necessary purchases for their trip without a guide, signing for them with a brand new credit card issued in the name of Rachel Davenport. In keeping with the pastoral setting they'd visit, she chose the trousseau of a passionate shepherdess: full, flowered skirts and lacy petticoats, tucked lawn blouses cut to show off a lush curve of bosom and slender suntanned arms.

She wanted no slinky satin pajamas or traditional peignoir for their wedding night. Instead she would give herself to Marcus in a simple airy shift of pin-tucked cotton batiste, edged with lace delicate enough for a baby's christening gown.

Once her shopping was completed, the days of waiting seemed infinite. Rachel found herself suffering from an acute attack of nerves. Yet though she awoke several times from a sound sleep to wonder if Marcus would show up for the ceremony, she couldn't bring herself to check on his whereabouts.

Maybe he's changed his mind, she told herself repeatedly. I'll get a check in the mail along with his apologies—or a telegram from the Orient, canceling all our plans.

There was no one to talk with about her fears. Her mother was long dead, and there wouldn't be any bridesmaids. Her few friends and female relatives were thousands of miles distant. Each time she was tempted to phone one of them, she realized how difficult—and embarrassing—it might be to explain the terms of her engagement. To complicate matters further, she didn't want her father to know about her marriage until after the ceremony. She suspected famed evangelist Luther Vanden would be highly critical of her plans.

Desperate for activity of any kind, Rachel tried to immerse herself in her painting. It helped, though not as much as she'd hoped.

Shortly after noon on the day before the wedding, Marcus finally phoned. "I'm back in London," he informed her, his voice clipped and formal. "I trust everything is full speed ahead."

"As far as I know," she responded softly. Barefoot, wearing her painting smock and jeans, she pushed back an unruly strand of dark hair.

"Good." The line hummed for a moment. "I wonder if I might send my car around for you," he said. "I was hoping we could meet at S.J. Phillips, on New Bond Street, to pick out your wedding and engagement rings. Afterward we can stop by my solicitor's."

In the first flush of emotion on hearing from him, she'd forgotten about their prenuptial contract.

"Give me half an hour," she said, unbuttoning her smock as she cradled the receiver against her shoulder. If she had *her* way, their marriage was going to last.

Jervis called for her in the Daimler, and Rachel noticed a new deference in his manner. This is actually happening, she thought, half-tempted to pinch herself as she was whisked across town to her destination. By tomorrow night Marcus and I will be married. I'll be Mrs. Marcus Davenport.

He met her at the curb outside the jeweler's shop. As usual he cut a striking figure, his dark hair lifting faintly in the breeze. She thought he looked tired and noted dark circles beneath his eyes and a shadow of a beard on his face. He's been working too hard, she thought, wanting to put her arms around him. He needs somebody to make him rest.

Placing a light kiss on her cheek, he led her inside the paneled showroom. As hushed and traditional as if it had been handed down all-of-a-piece from the Edwardian era, S.J. Phillips glittered like Ali Baba's cave with its displays of tiaras, silver plate and crystal.

An elderly clerk stepped forward to escort them to the diamond section. Rings, necklaces and bracelets worth a queen's ransom reposed on ruby velvet in their walnut-framed glass cases.

Politely ascertaining Rachel's size, the clerk made several discreet suggestions. None met with Marcus's approval. Asking to see a beautiful but cold-looking solitaire set in platinum, he slipped it on her finger.

The ring was a perfect fit. "Well? What do you think?" he asked.

Flushing, Rachel wondered if the clerk had noticed his matter-of-fact tone. "It's lovely," she answered. "But so...so *large*. I'm sure it must be worth a fortune."

"I want you to have the best."

Casually signing the credit slip, Marcus asked the clerk to box up the matching wedding band. It didn't surprise her when he failed to choose a similar ring for himself. Before she could catch her breath or even think about what was happening, he was ushering her into the Jaguar.

"Now for the solicitor's," he said, as if checking off an agenda item.

Marcus's legal representative was a thin balding man who peered incuriously at Rachel through gold-rimmed half spectacles. He showed no emotion as he handed each of them a copy of the marriage contract. Maybe to him this is an accepted way of doing business, Rachel thought as her pen scratched across the final page of each copy. He probably doesn't realize his ironclad phrases could bar any possibility of love and trust.

Marcus begged off dinner when they arrived back at her flat. Looking genuinely weary and complaining of jet lag, he reminded her they'd be spending the next few weeks together. Meantime he needed to get some sleep.

"If it's all right with you," he said, "I'll pick you up about nine-thirty tomorrow morning. We'll drive over to the registry together."

She nodded. They regarded each other for a moment without speaking.

"Perhaps you'd like to come up for a glass of sherry," she suggested finally. "You needn't stay long. But we really do have something to celebrate."

To her pleasant surprise, Marcus agreed readily. "You're right, of course. I should have thought to bring champagne."

Rachel's new diamond reflected tiny pinpoints of light as she poured out the drinks. Then, sitting beside Marcus on a lumpy divan, she invited him to offer a toast.

"To happiness," he answered promptly. "And the success of all our plans."

They clinked their glasses. Sipping at her sherry, Rachel listened quietly while Marcus talked of his latest business accomplishments and his intention of flying them to Brittany himself in the company plane.

Nothing prepared her for the suddenness with which he stood and drained his glass—or for the way he pulled her to her feet. Sensing his rough urgency, she had no way of knowing how her delicate perfume had inflamed his senses, making him want to lean closer and bury his face in her neck.

During his absence from England, Rachel's image had repeatedly crossed his mind. He'd thought of her in business meetings and crowded hotel bars, during dinner with friends and going through profit-and-loss statements. Most of all, he'd thought of her late at night. Despite his reputation as a playboy, it had been a long time since he'd made love to anyone.

Does she have any notion how tantalizing she is? he wondered, frowning down at her now in the modest little flat. Or realize how delectable she looks in that soft sheer blouse? Even the luminous single strand of pearls she's wearing only emphasizes her womanly curves.

"As taxing as the past two weeks have been," he confessed, his voice a low growl of frustration, "I haven't been able to get you out of my mind."

"Nor I you."

The halting admission was more than he could take. With a little groan he claimed her mouth, bruising it with the sudden ferocity of his kisses. In response she seemed to melt into him.

Her sweet submission was like a match to tinder. Half-mad with wanting her, Marcus fumbled for her buttons. A moment later his hand was beneath her blouse, pushing aside her bra and closing possessively over one lush and yielding breast.

The sensation created by his thumb as he rubbed it back and forth across her nipple sent shivers racing to her very core. A deep craving settled in her most private places. Only he could ease it by merging their separate selves.

Never had she wanted—*needed* a man so much. Desperate with arousal and inflamed by his readiness, Rachel dug her fingers into his shoulders. With every shred of her being, she longed to give him what he wanted: the complete surrender that was her own dearest wish.

To her acute distress, long-held principles got in the way. "Please..." she begged, pushing lightly against him. "We can't do this, Marcus. It isn't right." He didn't know she was fighting a perilous battle against herself.

"Are you sure this is what you want?" he asked. Blunt sarcasm masked his hurt at what he took for rejection. Marcus caught up the hand that displayed his diamond. "Better make certain you're ready for what this ring signifies."

Still flushed with the heat of arousal, Rachel took a step back from him. God help me but I *am* ready for it, she thought, doing up her buttons.

He seemed to be waiting for some kind of answer.

"Don't worry," she promised breathlessly, hoping he couldn't read her thoughts. "I'll be as compliant as even you could wish, Marcus Davenport...*after* tomorrow's ceremony."

They wed at a registry late the following morning, with the magistrate's wife and son serving as witnesses. Rachel emerged with her new husband to be swarmed by Britain's sensationalist press.

By midafternoon, headlines touted the union of a wealthy British financier and ladies' man with Luther Vanden's daughter. "Office Romance," one tabloid screamed. "Father Not Invited to Wedding," another proclaimed. The photographers with their zoom lenses had faithfully caught Marcus's scowl and a stunned-looking Rachel ducking into the Daimler with an armload of roses.

They lunched at the Savoy, having poached salmon, caviar, and champagne in the Grill Room. On their way home to Belgravia, Marcus stopped the car so he could purchase several tabloids from a newsboy.

"Damn the leeches!" he muttered, quickly reviewing one of the most scurrilous papers, which focused at length on his alleged romantic exploits. He swore even more roundly at another, which hinted Rachel had been having an affair with him even before her late husband's death.

For her part, Rachel could only shake her head. Now that the news had hit the streets, it would be on television and radio broadcasts in the States. Her father, who rose early, would probably hear it before much time had passed. Fervently she hoped they'd be out of London before he tracked her down with an angry phone call.

She was not to get her wish. On their arrival at Marcus's elegant nineteenth-century town house, the butler informed them that "Mrs. Davenport's father is on the phone."

Picking up the receiver in her new husband's study, Rachel listened quietly for several minutes, letting her father's ire run its course. His accusations that Marcus was a reprobate and that she'd embarrassed Des's family by marrying again so quickly didn't faze her. She wasn't surprised when, after several minutes, her father's objections took on a more narrow focus: the fact that she'd be remaining in England now, not coming back home to North Carolina to help with his crusades.

Finally, just as Marcus joined her to sit and listen from the corner of his leather-topped desk, she spoke her mind. Politely but firmly she told her father to butt out of her affairs.

"Whether or not I married Marcus, Dad," she said, "I had no intention of coming back to the States. Or, for that matter, of working with you again. This is something I want, and I hope you'll get used to it. Maybe even get around to wishing us happiness." Adding a polite goodbye she hung up the phone.

The flight to France was like no other she'd known. Alone on the twin-engine Lear jet with Marcus, she sat in the copilot's seat, marveling at his expertise with all the dials and equipment. For the first time, I feel like a bride, she thought, burying her face in the roses she still carried. We even look like newlyweds—me in my ivory suit and he in his dark one, with a blush-pink rosebud in his lapel.

Once they'd cleared the tower and begun heading south over West Sussex toward the English Channel, she could feel Marcus relax by inches. Clearly he loved flying. He gave her a brilliant grin as they moved out over water, far above its glimmering sheen of sunlight, amid a flock of puffy white clouds.

"Great day for this, isn't it?" he asked, not seeming to expect an answer. "Being up here makes me realize how good it is to be alive."

To Rachel's delight their route took them over the Conentin Peninsula and that wonder of the Western world, the islanded abbey-fortress of Mont-Saint-Michel. At her exclamation of pleasure, Marcus dropped their altitude so she could have a closer look. The tide was out, and the rocky mount with its slate-roofed church and bristling spires cast pointed blue shadows over a bay of glistening quicksand. Rivulets that had trapped the ocean's waters reflected the sunlight.

The afternoon was running out like sand in an hourglass by the time they landed at the Quimper airport. Checking through customs and transferring their luggage to a rental car, they quit the city for country roads bordered by fields and ever more-scattered cottages. Here and there stood dark copses of trees.

Rachel could smell the sea as they turned into a grassy sunken lane between wooded banks. She caught her breath moments later at the stark beauty of Marcus's cottage. Flanked by twin chimneys and huddled beneath a steep roof of blue-gray slate, the rectangular whitewashed stone dwelling was set high enough to have a view of the water. Low hedges and a few straggling trees barely disrupted the sweep of sea and sky.

"Marcus, it's wonderful!" she exclaimed. "So isolated and peaceful. Yet you feel it could ride out any storm."

Her rhapsodizing drew a quick smile from the dark-haired man beside her. "Better take a closer look before deciding whether or not you like it," he advised. "The place isn't blessed with modern conveniences. You might find it a bit too rugged for your taste."

The caveat did little to blunt her enthusiasm as they carried in their bags. Someone, she saw, had been there before them, throwing the windows open to the mild salt air and sweeping the flagstone floors until they were spotless. Cold meat, cheese, a crock of butter and a round crusty loaf of bread reposed on a table next to the stone fireplace. Beside them, a jug of cider was still cool to the touch.

"I allow a neighboring farmer free use of my fields," Marcus explained in answer to her questioning look. "When they can, he and his family repay the favor."

Rachel gazed about her in fascination. She'd heard of the famous box beds of Brittany—tall richly carved wooden cabinets containing straw-and-feather mattresses, with attached linen chests that served as a kind of step for entering them. But she hadn't expected to see a pair of such beds opposite the kitchen hearth.

Marcus gave her an indulgent look. "Don't worry," he reassured her. "Those old things are just curiosities. We'll be sleeping in the other room."

Their mood shifted at the mention of sleeping arrangements. Suddenly awkward with each other, they put their things away in the tiny breeze-swept bedroom. Inevitably their eyes met over its most striking furnishing, a giant four-poster with freshly tucked linen sheets.

How must she feel, Marcus thought, giving herself to me simply because she wants a baby? Suddenly and fiercely he hoped it was more than that. For her sake, as well as his own, he hoped the passionate response he'd felt several times wasn't simply in his imagination.

Thinking how much she loved him now, Rachel had her own fears. What if she couldn't please him, make him feel what other women had? Despite her marriage to Des, she was inexperienced. Des had been her only partner and he had never really introduced her to the art of love.

Wishing he could read her thoughts, Marcus peeled off his jacket and tie. "You might want to put on something more comfortable," he suggested, nodding at her arrow-slim skirt and delicate high heels. "After supper I thought we might take a walk."

She joined him in the kitchen several minutes later wearing a flowered skirt, short-sleeved blouse and espadrilles. Tossing a shawl she planned to wear later over the back of the chair, she arranged her roses in a tall earthenware crock that Marcus had filled with water from a pump. Inhaling a deep whiff of their hothouse scent, she got out plates and prepared a simple meal. The bread, cheese and cider were delicious, but neither she nor Marcus seemed to have much appetite.

"Come on," he told her, getting to his feet. "We can leave these things until later. The sunset won't last."

They walked to a low promontory overlooking the water. Beyond it stretched a deserted tan beach. There wasn't another dwelling in sight. Seabirds waded in gleaming eddies, and the sky was streaked with rose as if from a giant's paint box.

Yet the scene was anything but tranquil. Huge Atlantic breakers roiled and flattened, battering then tugging at the prow of a continent. Stiff breezy gusts of wind blew Rachel's skirt against her legs.

How I love it here, she thought, drawing her shawl more closely about her shoulders. To her, the moisture-laden air was exhilarating and almost electrically charged. The hiss and boom of the surf drummed in her ears like a heartbeat.

Afterward she couldn't have said how long they stood side by side but not touching, thinking their separate thoughts. Her past seemed to dangle by a thread as the sun slowly sank below the horizon. The low promontory became a jumping-off point, the verge of a different life.

Finally most of the light had gone. With a casual gesture, as if they were lovers of long-standing, Marcus slipped an arm about her waist.

"It's been a long day," he remarked softly, pressing the hand that bore his wedding ring to his lips. "If you have no objection, Rachel, perhaps we should turn in for the night."

# Chapter Seven

Unlike the previous afternoon, Marcus didn't seem inclined to play the aggressor. Instead he lingered on the cottage stoop, smoking a last cigarette as the twilight deepened and giving her time to change in the privacy of their room.

Barefoot in her batiste gown, Rachel brushed her hair into a shoulder-length halo of dark curls. In the fading light she could see the shadowy shape of her body—slender waist, curving hips, dark-smudged nipples faintly visible through the semitransparent fabric.

Whatever happens later, I'll be his, she thought, a little flame of desire curling to life inside her. And he'll be mine. If I have his baby, we'll always be part of each other. She grew hot and cold all over, thinking of what the night could bring.

Certain he expected her to slip beneath the covers and wait for him, she decided on a different approach. For a moment she stood unobserved on the cool flagstones of the kitchen, memorizing the way he looked lounging in the low entryway, his powerful figure silhouetted against the gathering dusk. Then, stealing up behind him, she placed her hand lightly on his arm as if to claim him.

Surprised from his thoughts, Marcus turned to face her. His dark blue eyes glittered with the first swift stirrings of desire.

Tossing his cigarette aside, he swept her up in his arms. She's light as a feather, he thought in amazement. Yet so warm and womanly, all curves, tender hollows and delicious places. The trusting way her bare arms were twined about his neck made him want to protect her with his life—even while he ravaged her very essence.

"Can you have any idea how much I've wanted you?" he asked, his rough voice catching on the words. "For the past two weeks, I've thought of little else but covering you with my body. Kissing you until your skin's on fire with it. *Sowing life in you,* as you once so vividly suggested."

The erotic confession tumbled the last barriers in her mind. Primitive female response soared uppermost. "Take me, then," she urged, offering herself without reservation. "I promise I won't hold anything back."

He didn't need a second invitation. Carrying her through the kitchen, he set her down gently on the edge of the four-poster. Her eyes widened as, half-kneeling in front of her, he ran his hands lightly over her body, learning its shape.

"You're so lovely," he whispered, bending to kiss her feet, then blazing a path up her calves as he pushed up her gown. "I could devour you completely with what I feel."

"Yes, Marcus, yes..."

Crying out with pleasure as he kissed her knees and her thighs and praised their silken softness, Rachel meshed her fingers in his dark hair. She wanted to laud his body in return, longed to confess to this man who was now her husband that her need was as great as his.

Words failed her as he buried his face against her stomach, reaching up to plunder her breasts. Sharp flickers of need sped through her. The deliberate, gentle pressure of his thumbs against her nipples was igniting her body.

In a rage to have him, she finished taking off the gown herself. Naked to his gaze and the cool sea-scented air, she cupped her breasts to offer them like ripe fruit.

The welcoming gesture twisted a knife of pleasure deep inside him. Moments later she was moaning at the unspeakable luxury of it as his mouth closed over one rosy peak.

Determined to draw out their mutual pleasure, Marcus teased her tight pink bud lightly at first. The thought that his child would similarly nuzzle at her honeyed breasts defeated him. Unable to help himself, he intensified his demand.

Awash in feeling, Rachel tried unsuccessfully to pull him up with her on the bed.

Go easy, he cautioned himself, lifting his head to look at her. Don't give in and take her yet. But a hot ache had settled in his groin, and he was burning up as with a fever. He didn't know how long he could last.

Frustrated in her attempt, Rachel reached for his buttons. "*Please*, Marcus," she whispered, trying to work them loose from their buttonholes.

In response his eyes held a smoldering question.

"I want to feel you. Please, take off your things," Rachel said softly.

He surrendered with a groan. His fingers brushing against hers, he removed his shirt to reveal the inverted triangle of dark chest hair she remembered. Next came his belt, to be quickly tossed aside. She caught her lip between her teeth as his trousers and shorts followed, baring his taut readiness.

Time stood still as he towered over her, searing her with his gaze. My God, but she's beautiful, he thought. So delicate and yet so tempting with that tiny waist and those come-hither eyes. I want to make love to her until we both drop from exhaustion.

Easing her back against the coverlet, he lay down beside her. Eagerly she enfolded him, stroking the broad muscles of his back, then daring to reach lower for the long lean curve of his hips and buttocks. Just the freedom to touch him that way set off spreading ripples of delight. I could die now, she thought, knowing what happiness is.

A moment later she realized the extent of her naïveté. Feathering little kisses along her throat, he smoothed one hand down the flat curve of her stomach to part her thighs. Then and only then, as he awakened her to quivering life, did she begin to guess what it was to be a woman, freed of her ghosts and on the brink of making love to Marcus, a man who was bent on satisfying her most sensuous claims.

I want to be wife...mother...courtesan for his pleasure, Rachel thought, each image abetting the frenzied rhythm he was beginning to evoke. As deep as the earth and as wide as the sea for him. An infinite vessel to hold the full measure of his desire.

Closing her eyes, she let the feeling take her, bearing her up and up into realms of delight that had no boundaries, whole kingdoms of bliss inhabited only by his touch. From moment to moment her ravenous response threatened to sweep her past the outer limits of experience, beyond every barrier she'd ever known.

Suddenly she broke free, cries of astonishment escaping her as release came in little shudders; its heat permeated her like a rush of flame. Gradually a delicious ache settled in her thighs, making them feel heavy, languid. She relaxed then, her hips sinking back to the bed.

I never knew it could be this way, she thought, holding fast to him. Never dreamed it, not in my wildest imagination.

Cradling her, stroking her, Marcus was similarly overcome. It's her first time, he realized in amazement. No one but me has ever done this for her.

The thought was enough to return him to aching readiness. Not yet, he cautioned himself, smoothing her hair and kissing the bare curve of her shoulder. Let her explore her marvelous new discovery to the utmost.

Her awareness settling to earth again, Rachel repudiated his forbearance. "Marcus," she began, realizing suddenly that he'd put her satisfaction before his own. "You haven't—"

"Hush." Lightly, he laid one finger against her lips. "I want you to go with the flow of what you're feeling."

"I am. Oh, I am. Please, fill me," she whispered.

He couldn't bring himself to refuse her sweet demand. Repeating her name as if it were a talisman, he fitted himself to her body. Briefly he held her motionless, as if the slightest friction would bring a too-swift reward.

Lying thus, with the weight of his body pressing her into the mattress, Rachel was astonished anew. A sensual neophyte, she'd thought the release she'd just experienced was love's universe. Yet the very fullness of him now was enough to reawaken her need.

I want him in every way there is, she thought, exulting in the unsuspected depth and breadth of her womanhood. Not just as a vessel but as a crucible. This time we'll burn to ashes together.

Marcus's face was a mask of wanting in the darkened room as he slowly began to move. Instinctively she followed, falling into a complementary rhythm that was as natural as breathing.

This time she reached her summit just seconds before he did. Her cataclysm was as different from the first as night from morning—deep and implosive, drowning her in huge waves of pleasure that rocked her to the soles of her feet. It was as if the earth and the stars fell away, leaving just the two of them free-falling in the universe.

In that moment, Rachel's sense of connectedness to Marcus was overwhelming. Mutely she gloried in the shiver of gooseflesh that swept over his back and shoulders.

We're like every man and woman who've made love since the beginning of time, she thought as he collapsed against her. We're joined to them in our communion, an intimate part of the earth.

For what seemed an eternity, they didn't stir, electing to lie there with their bodies all tangled together. The sounds of waves in the distance softly reported the sea's unseen presence. The night air filled the room, and somewhere a bird called sleepily, then fell silent.

At last Marcus rolled over to lie beside her. "Are you happy?" he asked gruffly, gathering her back into his arms.

"Yes, happy," she whispered. If only she dared to tell him everything she felt. But she didn't. "Maybe you guessed," she said, risking a small part of it. "I've never...*gone wild* that way before, during lovemaking."

"Yes, I did guess that," he admitted.

"And you don't mind? About my inexperience, I mean?"

In response he uttered a little oath. "Good Lord, Rachel," he exclaimed. "Don't you realize I feel privileged, sweetheart? In a way, you came to me untouched."

Spontaneously offered, the endearment was like a boon. Eagerly Rachel hugged it to her heart. Dreams of making him love her as she loved him were floating through her mind as they drifted into sleep.

She felt bereft when she awoke many hours later in a stream of sunlight to find him gone.

"Marcus?" she called, half expecting him to step back through the low doorway leading to the kitchen with morning coffee on a tray.

There wasn't any answer. Throwing off the bed covers, she retrieved her nightdress to go looking for him. But the cottage had few hiding places, and he wasn't anywhere to be found.

With a little knot of uneasiness forming in her stomach, she put on her skirt, blouse and espadrilles. I hope he isn't sorry about what happened between us last night, she thought, stepping out to the dooryard with its straggling ornamental plantings of hydrangeas. Or that, on reflection, he doesn't view the rightness of our coming together as an emotional trap.

One of her mental questions was quickly answered: he hadn't really gone. Their rental car was still parked securely at the end of the lane.

Retracing their footsteps of the night before, she started down the path toward the water. It was going to be a lovely morning. Already the sun was warm on her arms.

Emerging from the little track with its low hedges, she spotted her new husband's solitary figure. He was seated on a big flat rock, his dark brows knit together in a frown as he stared pensively out to sea. As she hesitated, he glanced in her direction.

"I wondered where you were," she said, feeling a bit foolish as she crossed the space between them.

He shrugged. "I woke up with the sun and couldn't get back to sleep."

Rachel fought the urge to put her arms around him. "Is everything all right?" she asked.

He reached for her hand, and suddenly it was as if his remote mood had never existed.

"This godforsaken coast brings out the Breton in me, I suppose," he admitted, his dark blue eyes crinkling at her in the brilliant sunlight. "You mustn't take it personally, Rachel. What do you say we fix ourselves some breakfast? And then explore?"

Despite her uncertainty and Marcus's habit of distancing himself after intimate contact, the next few days proved to be a lyrical time for both of them. Freed of the nervousness that had lain between them on their wedding night, they made love again that afternoon in a pasture full of wildflowers, bombarded by bees and laughing uproariously when a hay wagon passed in the lane.

"The poor driver!" Rachel exclaimed, delighted at her own risqué behavior. "He must be positively scandalized."

Marcus shook his head. "Not a chance," he advised in a licentious tone, nibbling with gusto on her ear. "This is France, you know. And anyway, he couldn't see us."

"Maybe not *most* of us," she laughed, wriggling her toes behind the nape of his neck. "But what about my feet? They're not the sort of thing one expects to see sprouting up out of a field!''

A moment later their mirth turned back into longing. Never had Rachel guessed desire could be so thoroughly satisfied yet revived within minutes—even more powerfully than before.

The realization was confirmed again that night as she and Marcus came together again in greater sureness and even more passion. The next day found them deep in each other's embrace after jumping into a hayloft together.

Happier than she'd ever thought possible, Rachel contentedly pulled straws from her hair as they walked back to the cottage, deeply pleased to discover that her new husband had a lighthearted, even joyous, side. Except for his retreat to the beach on the first morning of their honeymoon, his dark moods seemed to have vanished without a trace.

I could stay here in Brittany with him forever, she thought, lying beside him one night after making love. We could raise our children here. I wouldn't care if I ever saw anything but this lovely isolated stretch of coast.

As the week lengthened, her love for Marcus grew, though no words of caring were exchanged between them. For her part, Rachel didn't dare to speak about what she felt. Instinctively she guessed their relationship was still fragile. Any declaration of affection might cause him to retreat.

Still, encouraged by his mood and the warmth of
his lovemaking, she began to feel more confident
that the uncertainties between them would be resolved. In the meantime she hoped the language of
touch would suffice. Willingly she adopted its vo-
cabulary, offering him caresses that were like love
poems, explicit and passionate epics of what was in
her heart.

The day they set off on borrowed horses for a
nearby village fair near the end of their first week
together promised to be another pearl on an unbro-
ken string. In honor of the fine weather—sunny and
mild with a light breeze off the ocean—Rachel wore
a white ruffled skirt and blouse and tied a blue sash
about her waist.

Marcus noticed how vividly the outfit set off her
tan as he helped her into the saddle. Her shapely
brown legs dangled from beneath her pushed-up skirt
and the shorts she wore beneath it for modesty's
sake, causing him to think about making love to her
again.

In high spirits he laughed and teased her as they
rode, seemingly eager to show her the surrounding
countryside. Briefly they halted at a small *calvaire*,
a sort of rustic shrine built into a cobblestoned niche,
adorned with a crucifix and crude folk carvings of
various saints. Several bouquets, now withered, had
been placed at its foot.

Such shrines were the modern equivalent of the
dolmens and Celtic crosses they'd passed on their

way from Quimper the afternoon of their arrival, Marcus explained.

"The more Brittany changes, the more she stays the same," he said, paraphrasing the French proverb. "No doubt you'll hear snatches of ancient Breton being spoken in the village this afternoon."

After spending so much time in isolation at the cottage, the festival sponsored by Sts. Anne et Yves parish, with its exuberant crowd of villagers dressed in traditional garb, offered just the right degree of sociability. Rachel, who had brought her camera in hope of snapping some local scenes to paint, found a wealth of worthy subjects.

The women were prim and festive in their gold-embroidered black dresses with snowy aprons and starched caps, and they enchanted her. So did the children. Fitted out in their Sunday best, the boys wore dark jackets and broad-brimmed hats while the girls preened in more colorful versions of their mothers' attire.

Admiring them and the apple-cheeked babies, Rachel tried to imagine the child she and Marcus would create. I can't understand how his first wife could cheat on him, she thought, even if the press of business called him away from her now and then. Surely moments like the ones we've shared would be worth occasional loneliness.

Intrigued by her thoughtful expression, Marcus caught her by the hand. Eagerly they joined the crowd lining a narrow cobbled street just as the religious parade started. To Rachel's amazement, the standard bearers with their richly emblazoned banners and statues of the saints were followed by bagpipers in beribboned hats and black waistcoats with velvet collars. The fierce keening of their pipes, accompanied by brass instruments Marcus called *bombardons*, had an almost Scottish flavor.

Following the singing of several hymns in modern-day French, the parade wound with much pomp and ceremony to the church's south porch, where a priest held forth with a brief sermon and blessing.

At last the secular festival could begin. Pipes were abandoned for fiddles and accordians, and the villagers began to dance in a cleared area beneath the trees. Appearing as if by magic, the local wine flowed freely. Children darted about, permitted for once to indulge in their pranks.

Flower sellers set up shop, as did a potter hawking examples of famed Quimper tableware, hand-decorated in rustic eighteenth-century motifs. Unable to resist some scalloped plates and oddly shaped cups and saucers patterned in cream, russet and blue, Rachel gave Marcus a helpless look.

"Wedding present," he grinned, peeling off the required number of franc notes and asking that their purchase be forwarded to the Quimper airport.

She was a bit light-headed from several unaccustomed glasses of wine when her new husband asked her to dance. A bit hesitantly she rested one hand on his shoulder and placed her other hand in his. But though she'd had as little experience with dancing as she'd had with alcohol, he was an excellent partner. She felt light and graceful in his arms.

It's as if we were meant to dance together, she thought giddily, as he whirled her about the dusty common under the trees. It's the same when we make love. Though we're just beginning to discover each other, we move like one person.

When the number ended, Marcus didn't release her. Instead, his eyes glinting at her mischievously, he leaned down to kiss her mouth.

Several approving murmurs from the crowd made Rachel blush. But she couldn't help smiling back at one wrinkled old man, tieless in a threadbare suit with a blue knit cap pulled over his ears, who gave her a conspiratorial wink.

As a people, the Bretons had seemed quite conservative to Rachel. Mentally she'd compared them with some of the more traditional members of her father's Greensboro congregation—good-hearted but not given to public displays of affection.

Now, as the music started up again for a country *gavotte* and Marcus held out his hands, she realized she hadn't known the full story. Bretons were Frenchmen, too, as Marcus had pointed out. Being part French, perhaps Marcus had the same hidden effusiveness.

They were nearly ready to leave the festival later that afternoon, when the weather abruptly changed. Suddenly the air smelled of approaching rain.

Looking up, Rachel was surprised to note the sky's ominous slate-blue color.

Almost simultaneously Marcus slipped and called her "my love." Instantly he was remote and cold, the sunlight gone from his face. Yet though he'd clamped down on them with all the considerable force of his being, he was plainly seething with tumultuous emotions.

"Let's go," he suggested in the kind of tone he might use to address a stranger.

Rachel felt chilled as he helped her into the saddle. The very idea that he might learn to care for me is enough to drive him away, she thought. All I can do is keep loving him, but I don't know how to fight his ghosts.

A heavy ache had settled near her heart, but she had little time for introspection. Setting a breakneck pace, Marcus made it almost impossible for her to keep up with him. The pounding of her own mare's hooves as they ground up the dirt road leading back toward the cottage jarred her half-senseless.

With a shout Marcus turned off just as they reached the crest of a hill. Galloping after him, Rachel saw that the grassy lane he'd chosen led directly to the shore.

They hit the hard-packed beach at a furious clip, tearing up clots of wet sand as they turned to follow the line of breakers. Already the wind had picked up, heralding the approaching storm.

At the speed they rode, it took only a short time to reach the stretch of beach that fronted on their cottage. Abruptly Marcus wheeled about, reaching for her horse's reins. Lathered and spent, the animal balked.

"What... what is it?" Rachel cried.

*"I want you."*

Jumping from the saddle, he was beside her in an instant, reaching for her waist. A moment later he was dragging her down into his arms.

Their horses trotted off toward higher ground, but she didn't notice. Crushing her to him, he caressed her breasts. At the same time, his free hand was under her skirt, pushing up her petticoat.

In a flash she realized what was happening. Desperately she tried to pull away as he tugged at the button placket of her shorts.

*"No!"* She gasped, her shock and hurt reverberating in little echoes. "Please, Marcus... not like this!"

Her words had absolutely no effect. Silencing them with his mouth, he pulled her down with him on the sand so that they lay half in the surf. Foam flecked, the greediest waves reached up to lap against them.

He was her husband, after all. And she loved him. Yet, stricken by the savage tenor of his lovemaking, Rachel tried to fight.

She was no match for her own attraction to him. She began to gradually want him as much as he wanted her. Fingers that had pushed against him relented and furtively began to caress. With a little moan of defeat, she helped him strip off her shorts.

Even if she lived to be a hundred, Rachel thought she would never forget the way Marcus took her that day or the way she welcomed him with fierce, almost violent hunger as her tears mixed with the taste of sea salt against her tongue. Her cheeks would grow hot, remembering how shudders had racked her as he'd claimed his reward.

Afterward she simply collapsed with him, her chest heaving in ragged gulps. Mutely he pressed against her, as if his body were made of lead.

Moments seemed stretched to hours by the time he moved off her and stood. In response, Rachel pulled down her crumpled skirt to cover herself. She could only guess how daunted and vulnerable she looked, her nipples still rigid against the wet fabric of her blouse.

Marcus stared at her with reluctant fascination. I don't want to love her, he thought. I can't afford that kind of anguish again.

At last he spoke.

"If we didn't manage to create life in you that time," he said, his tone biting, "the next couple of years will probably be wasted effort."

Hurtful though it was, Rachel felt the remark was oddly directed against himself.

## Chapter Eight

After their lovemaking on the beach, the cottage seemed too small to hold them. Barricading herself behind the closed door of their room, Rachel flung her ruined clothing down in a heap. Naked, she wielded her hairbrush with vigor, determined to remove every trace of sand and grit from her tangled tresses.

Her body felt bruised and tingling, permanently branded by the force of Marcus's lovemaking. As reason returned, however, she was forced to admit the truth: dangerous roughness on his part had been purely emotional. Though she'd struggled with him, he hadn't hurt her in the slightest—or even left a mark.

Injured by his callousness, yet as deeply in love with him as ever, she felt nothing but scorn for her own behavior. Do you think it will teach him tenderness? she asked herself as she washed her face with water from a large ironstone pitcher.

Emerging some minutes later in slacks and a high-necked sweater, she saw that it was already spitting rain. Marcus was in the dooryard, talking with a neighbor youth who had bicycled over to bring him a telegram.

"I have to fly to Paris tonight and oversee Air Anglia operations there," he said, turning to Rachel with a troubled look. "One of our planes has been hijacked in Cairo. They're demanding the release of several political prisoners being held by the French government."

Shocked at the news, she didn't answer. Our idyll is ending, she thought. And not just in a figurative sense.

Turning back to the youth, Marcus made what appeared to be a series of requests in rapid-fire French. With a frown Rachel tried unsuccessfully to keep up with him. She guessed the subject had something to do with herself.

*"Oui, Monsieur Davenport,"* the boy replied several times, adding finally, *"Ne soyez pas inquiet, monsieur. Nous la garderons bien."*

"You can come with me or not...just as you choose," Marcus informed her as their visitor cycled furiously up the lane ahead of the coming storm.

"I'd prefer the former, of course. But Jean-Louis and his family will look after you if you decide to stay."

Still smarting from his comments on the beach, Rachel was stung afresh by his laissez-faire attitude. "I'm amazed that you would want my company," she retorted, one hand on her hip. "Does it involve the continued transaction of our personal business, by any chance?"

The gibe provoked a genuine flash of anger. Swiftly he brought it under control. "Something like that," he replied, giving her a condescending look as he went back inside the cottage to pack his things.

To Rachel, the wall he'd erected only exacerbated her emotional wounds. She was tempted to stay on at the cottage just to spite him. Still, she was unwilling that they go their separate ways. Instinctively she guessed that if she let him go now, he'd be absent from her life for quite a while.

Sadness descended on her as they locked up the cottage and stowed their bags in the car. I wonder when we'll be back, she thought, fastening the belt on her raincoat. This proved to be a healing kind of place. In another week or two, a simple declaration of affection might have lost its power to hurt him.

Rain was beating against the windows of their plane as they took off for Roissy/Charles de Gaulle International Airport a half hour later. Flying mostly by instruments, Marcus didn't seem inclined toward conversation and Rachel didn't want to distract him.

She was surprised when, after they'd landed and taxied across the wet tarmac to the terminal, he invited her to accompany him upstairs to Air Anglia Operations, where events in Cairo were being closely monitored. Nursing seemingly endless cups of coffee, Rachel looked on and listened for the better part of a tense night. Marcus's shirtsleeves were soon rolled up to reveal tanned forearms. He remained in the thick of the action, occasionally speaking over the radio-telephone hookup with Cairo.

Dawn was breaking when they finally got the word: Egyptian police had resolved the crisis, and the entire group of hostages had been released unharmed. A cheer went up in the Air Anglia staging room. Several of the firm's Paris officials and technical personnel gave Marcus hugs of congratulation.

Dark smudges beneath his eyes and beard shadowing his jaw, Marcus turned to her. The strain imposed by long hours of worrying about each passenger on the hijacked plane was still painfully evident.

"Everything's going to be all right," he said, easing the tension in his shoulders as he held out her raincoat. "What do you say we clear out of here and get some rest?"

Paris was just waking up as they drove into the city proper amid a stream of vegetable trucks and suburbanites on bicycles, carrying home their morning *baguettes*. On impulse Marcus pulled over to the curb in a workingman's district, parking in front of a steamy little café.

"I know we're both tired," he said, glancing in her direction, "but we have to eat."

The *Coq d'Or* exuded the mingled aromas of frying sausages, coffee and tobacco smoke. It appeared to be patronized mostly by men—blue-shirted construction and sanitation workers, and the occasional gendarme or Metro conductor in his smart uniform.

Elbowing their way to a table, they drank several cups of strong chicory-flavored *café noir* while they waited for the cook to prepare his Parisian version of a bountiful English breakfast.

At first Marcus remained silent. Rachel guessed he was lost in thought over the crisis they'd just been through. Watching him, she speculated he might also feel somewhat awkward over their confrontation of the previous afternoon.

God knew she did. Though they'd been married for more than a week, they were still essentially strangers. I'm not sure what would erase the damage we did, she thought. Maybe tender lovemaking. But she knew even that leveler of all cares was likely to leave some unanswered questions.

Expelling a deep sigh that seemed designed to lift the weight of the world from his shoulders, Marcus lit a cigarette.

"What happened tonight is my particular bad dream," he confided, suddenly willing to bare at least a small part of his soul. "As chief executive of Air Anglia, I'm ultimately responsible for thousands of lives. Tonight wasn't our first incident. I'm afraid one day a hijacking will result in someone being killed. Maybe someone I care about."

Rachel frowned. "I can understand your concern," she answered sympathetically. "But I don't see how that could happen."

For a moment his eyes gave away their deepest secrets. "Remember the fake kidnapping attempt I told you about," he asked, "the one that resulted in my son's death? Well, something similar could happen. For real. I'm surprised none of the thugs and terrorists so prominent in the news today haven't tried to extort money from me personally via that route.

"*You* could be the target next time. Or the child you may already be carrying. I'm not sure I could live through that kind of hell again."

Their breakfast—orange juice, croissants fresh from the oven and an omelet generously studded with mushrooms—arrived. As they dug in, Rachel realized his fears were genuine, yet she doubted if they'd ever be realized. For the first time, she began to understand how protective he was likely to be of any child they might have.

After breakfast they drove to Marcus's Paris apartment, located in a stunning old building not far from the Champs Elysées. Rachel immediately felt like a guest. She dressed quickly for bed in the ivory pajamas she'd worn at the Nevilles' house party—

certain that this time, at least, nothing would happen between them.

To her astonishment Marcus reached for her the minute she turned out the light. His growth of beard lightly abrading her skin, he made swift love to her, then simply rolled over and went to sleep.

I wonder if I *am* pregnant, Rachel thought, lying awake beside him and resting one hand on her stomach. With one part of herself she hoped that was the case. Nothing would please her more than to bear Marcus's child.

Yet there was trepidation, too, at that very thought. A deep-seated fear that he would abandon their intimacy once his objective had been achieved rose in her.

I'd never do anything to stop what we both want, she thought. Or postpone it—even if that drives him away from me. I'll just have to take my chances.

Still subtly at odds with each other, Rachel and Marcus returned to London the following morning. The pace of Marcus's business dealings picked up immediately on their return to the city, almost without missing a beat.

As the days became weeks, their prescribed meeting ground seemed limited to two places—the occasional public function she attended as his wife and the passionate intimacy of her bed.

Unlike their common arrangement at the cottage, Marcus maintained separate sleeping quarters at his

Belgravia residence. Each night they bedded down together, invariably to make love, and by morning he was always gone.

During the day, Rachel was left largely to her own devices. The town house on Belgrave Square ran without her, thanks to Marcus's butler, Alistair Simonds, plus a housekeeper, a cook and several maids. Though Marcus had provided her with a brand new Japanese import car to scoot about town in, Jervis stood ready to chauffeur her in the Daimler when the master of the house didn't require his services.

Not one to occupy her time shopping and dining in fancy restaurants, Rachel kept busy with her painting, selling several more works through Trewitt's and beginning to earn herself a small reputation. She also volunteered at the Bowes Center three days a week.

Active as she was, she still longed for the closeness to her new husband that had blossomed so briefly only to vanish after the Breton parish festival. She began to think that if Marcus were ever to return her love, she'd know it when she awoke some morning to find him beside her after it was light.

One evening, though, she caught several glimpses of the man who'd been such an ardent companion on her honeymoon. Scheduled to join him and some of his business friends at an opera in Covent Garden, she was checking on her makeup in the gilt Regency mirror that graced their entry hall when Marcus came up behind her. Lightly he rested his hands on her shoulders, which were bared by the thin straps of her sapphire-blue crepe de chine dress.

"You're looking exceptionally lovely tonight," he whispered, bending down to place a lingering kiss on the curve of her neck. "And how fortunate that you should choose that color."

"Fortunate?"

Mystified, Rachel let herself lean back against him. Despite their nightly intimacy, which seemed only to grow in its soul-shattering intensity with the passage of time, even the slightest brush of his hands was enough to set her pulse racing. Just thinking about how handsome he looked in his immaculate white shirt and dinner jacket made her knees go weak.

He didn't explain in words. Watching her face reflected in the mirror, he reached into his inside jacket pocket to bring forth a handful of blue fire—a slender platinum rope knit up of sapphires and diamonds that sparkled like a galaxy of stars.

Before she realized what was happening, he was fastening the expensive necklace around her throat. From its center, a pendent formed by a huge midnight-blue stone encircled with diamonds just grazed the shadowy hollow between her breasts.

Rachel was awestruck. The slender dark-haired woman gazing back at her from the mirror looked as regal as a princess.

"Marcus, it's so beautiful!" she cried softly, clutching at his hands. "Is it . . . actually *real*?"

He laughed, his eyes more radiant than any gemstone at her pleasure.

"You hardly deserve less, my beautiful wife," he said, turning her around and lifting her chin to impart a deep and thorough kiss. "Tonight I shall be the envy of every man present."

The words seemed prophetic. Rachel, already bolstered by her experience as the wife of a political candidate, had gradually become more comfortable with their excursions into London society. Tonight she shone, glowing with a confidence and deep-seated loveliness that rivaled her fabulous necklace.

To her, the glittering sapphires that lay cool against her skin were a badge of Marcus's regard, or at least of his admiration. That, not the necklace itself, was what mattered to her most. Yet she couldn't deny she felt extraordinarily beautiful with it around her throat.

At Covent Garden she was surprised to be photographed for the society columns, thus being accorded the same celebrity status as her husband and the international beauties who'd formerly hung on his arm.

Later their party spent an hour or so at a London dance club where punk rock stars rubbed shoulders with sheiks, stockbrokers, Japanese tourists, and peers of the realm. Marcus looked on in tolerant amusement as she attracted the attention of several wealthy and powerful men.

He frowned a little when one of their fellow guests at the Nevilles' party, David Llewellyn, turned up and asked her to dance, but then he smiled. In her unfailing receptivity to his affection, Rachel had given him no cause for jealousy.

"I think old David's half in love with you," he remarked later when they were home alone together.

Seated at her dressing table in a lacy strapless bra and bikini panties, Rachel was about to unfasten her necklace before placing it in the bedroom safe. "You can't mean that," she said.

Marcus shrugged, removing his heavy gold cuff links. "I don't know why not. Alan is..."

"Alan?" Wide-eyed, she turned to face him. "Alan *who*?"

"Alan Travers, my assistant. No, don't laugh, I'm serious. He's remarked to me several times of late what a lovely glow you have. Almost as if she has her own private source of candlepower, he said a few days ago. Don't tell me those aren't smitten words."

Rachel shook her head. I wish *you* would say that kind of thing to me, she responded silently. What wouldn't I give to hear words like that from your lips? Again her fingers went to the clasp of her necklace.

Watching her, Marcus paused with his shirt half-open. "No," he said suddenly. "Don't take it off. I want to make love to you while you're wearing it.

I've thought of little else tonight but how lovely you would look, with nothing but my sapphires decorating your beautiful breasts.''

Shakily Rachel got to her feet. Her eyes shut with ecstasy as Marcus finished undressing her, unpinning her hair and running his hands admiringly over her body.

"All silk and velvet," he murmured, lightly stroking her nipples to aching readiness. "You're so delicious. The necklace is a fitting tribute." Moments later he was carrying her to the bed.

Rachel offered herself unconditionally, glorying in the tenderest, most deeply satisfying lovemaking she'd known since his mood change in the Breton churchyard. He's *mine*, she exulted as they reached a shattering climax together—at least for this private, delirious moment. Maybe even mine to last.

Typically Marcus had withdrawn from the emotional contact by the next morning. He was exceptionally remote for the next several weeks. Shutting herself up in the little studio Alistair Simonds had set up for her on the mansion's third floor, Rachel painted as if her life depended on it.

Two more paintings sold for even higher prices than before, and she used the money to help the Bowes Center. But the need there was great, and she realized her earnings weren't enough to bridge the gap.

As she finished picking up some toys one afternoon after a play session with several emotionally disturbed children, the center's director, Jocelyn Banks, stopped by to chat with her.

"You're looking tired." Rachel had spoken unthinkingly and bit her lip in distress.

The director smiled. "That's all right," she said. "I'm not offended. I suppose I have a right to look exhausted, what with staying up half the night balancing columns of figures—"

"Budget still a serious problem?"

Mrs. Banks nodded. "I'm afraid as of June first we shall be open just three days a week, unless one hundred twenty thousand pounds magically appears from somewhere. In fact, we should be lucky to manage with that sum."

"But that's terrible!" Rachel exclaimed, her mind racing.

Taking off her glasses, Mrs. Banks rubbed wearily at the bridge of her nose. "Things could be worse," she admitted. "Without dedicated volunteers like you, Mrs. Davenport, we should already have closed our doors. I want you to know we appreciate your efforts."

Driving home a short while later, Rachel was lost in thought. The center can't be allowed to cut back on services, she insisted to herself—not when it does so much good helping the children of low-income parents grow up in a safe, nurturing environment. I simply can't let that happen.

But she didn't have the kind of money Mrs. Banks needed unless she tapped her husband's bank account. And that was completely out of the question. In her opinion, until she presented Marcus with an heir, she hadn't any right to his money, not even to make a worthy contribution to charity.

The only thing of real value Rachel possessed in her own right was her sapphire necklace, and she couldn't bear to part with that. But I can seek a loan! she thought excitedly, turning onto Belgrave Square and pressing the automatic garage opener. I have collateral in my growing reputation as an artist. Ian Trewitt at the gallery will vouch for me, and I can repay the bank with the proceeds from my paintings.

Filling out a loan application the next day at the ornate and somewhat stuffy financial institution where Marcus maintained his personal account, Rachel was amazed at the effortlessness of things. Though she had scant experience in financial affairs, she'd understood bankers to be a cautious, somewhat skeptical lot. Yet after a brief call from the bank to Trewitt's to confirm her association with them, she walked out with the entire sum she'd requested.

Rachel suspected that her loan application had been approved partly on the strength of her relationship to Marcus, and that the call to Trewitt's had been merely a courtesy to set her at ease. But she didn't let herself think that there was anything unusual in her actions, or that when Marcus heard of them that he might strongly disapprove.

At the time she and Marcus were married, Rachel had considered the possibility that she might not conceive. But she hadn't considered that outcome a very likely one. She was extremely healthy, after all. And, as much as she wanted a baby, she couldn't believe life would deny her again.

As Marcus's wife and very much in love with him, she didn't let herself worry. There was enough on her mind already—painting, volunteering at the center, and coping with her problematic husband. It wouldn't do to place too much emphasis on immediate results. She didn't want to inhibit their love-making.

Besides, she had always been irregular. It followed that, initially, they might find it difficult to judge the success or failure of their efforts.

Studiously she avoided facing the real reason for her nonchalance—a deep fear that Marcus would turn from her once the reason for their marriage had been fulfilled. Rarely did it surface except as a fleeting concern when she drifted off to sleep.

Then one morning after they'd been married a little more than two and a half months, the truth hit her in a rush. She felt queasy from the moment she got out of bed, and all the gradual physical changes that had taken place in her body became glaringly apparent. Even the glow Marcus and apparently Alan had remarked about was a telltale sign.

I'm pregnant! she thought. Why didn't I see it before? I'm going to have Marcus's baby!

Hugging herself in her marble-and-tile bathroom, Rachel was overcome with happiness. At that very moment, her husband's child lay sheltered beneath her heart. Soon its tiny heart would beat. It would learn to suck its thumb in the haven of her womb. And she would thrill to the precious flutter of its movement. Already I love it so, she thought. As much as Marcus, though it has a totally different place in my heart.

Yet, overjoyed as she was, she couldn't ignore her sudden fear. What if Marcus turns on me when I tell him? she asked herself. I know he wants this baby as much as I do. But will he still want to sleep with me now that his deepest wish has been fulfilled?

Washing her face and changing into city clothes, Rachel went downstairs in search of Alistair Simonds. Discreetly she extracted the name of Marcus's family physician. Then she went back upstairs to call for an appointment.

Her visit to the doctor's office that afternoon was surprisingly brief. After a quick but thorough examination, the fatherly physician confirmed her speculation.

"Congratulations, Mrs. Davenport," he said, beaming at her through horn-rimmed glasses.

"You're a healthy young woman. You should have a beautiful healthy child."

Driving home, Rachel realized she'd have to tell Marcus right away. Already the doctor had estimated that she was nearly two months along. You can't wait, she told herself fiercely. As it is, he'll wonder why you didn't guess before.

That night at dinner there was very little conversation. Marcus seemed preoccupied, and Rachel lapsed into an awkward silence as she searched for the right way to tell him about the baby. Afterward they retired to the drawing room where they'd previously spent several quiet evenings together.

"I ran into a banker friend of mine at a board meeting this afternoon," he remarked, giving her an odd look.

"Oh?" Rachel replied. Distracted by her own worries, she had no idea what he was talking about.

A moment later he laid the whole story on the table. The banker, Geoffrey Worthington, had politely twitted him about his wife seeking a loan. The inference had been that Marcus didn't provide her with enough money. "With all your millions, old boy, it's not cricket to be stingy with the little lady," he'd said.

Rachel felt her cheeks grow red hot. She'd never thought her charitable urge could result in his embarrassment.

"I won't deny I borrowed the money," she said in a small voice. "I apologize if it's caused you any distress."

By now Marcus was on his feet. He shook his head as if her answer didn't make any sense. *Unlike Deirdre, she never seems to care about the money,* he thought. *Is she in some kind of trouble, then? Or is she just mercenary, after all?*

"What I don't understand is the *why* of things," he said, baffled and angry at being confronted that way by a business associate. "What on earth could you possibly want that I haven't already given you?"

Softly Rachel confessed that the loan was for the children's center. "I just couldn't let the place go under," she explained. "I planned to pay it back with the proceeds from my paintings."

Astounded at the truth, Marcus secretly mellowed. He was more relieved than he cared to admit that Rachel was still the unspoiled, almost selfless woman who'd begun to matter to him too much. Still he was annoyed that she hadn't come to him with her problem. Leaving off his pacing, he pulled her to her feet.

"Why didn't you ask me for the money?" he demanded roughly. "Or simply write a check? I've given you access to my personal checking account."

Upset by her faux pas and distraught over the fears that had plagued her since morning, Rachel heard only his anger. She didn't catch the softening in his tone or realize he might view her failure to rely on him as a form of personal rejection.

"I didn't have the right to do either of those things ... then," she blurted out. "Now that I've earned it, I wouldn't hesitate."

Again Marcus was thoroughly at a loss. "Earned it?" he asked, his frown deepening. "I don't understand what you mean."

Words tumbled out of Rachel in a rush. "By producing the heir you wanted," she said, her tone sharper than she'd intended. "That's right, Marcus. For nearly two months now, I've been carrying your child!"

*Chapter Nine*

She was going to have his baby! Marcus's face lit up, and he grasped her by the wrists.

Involuntarily Rachel shrank back from him. His joy is all for the success of the scheme, she thought miserably. Now that I'm pregnant, he won't want me anymore. Gratitude is the most I can expect.

Her instinctive withdrawal cut Marcus to the quick. His expression darkened. "Why didn't you tell me earlier?" he demanded, not even remotely guessing at what she felt.

Rachel's response was barely audible. "I . . . just confirmed it myself this morning."

He was silent a moment.

"So your part of the bargain is finished, and now you don't have to put up with my attentions, is that it?"

Suddenly realizing what was going through his mind, Rachel was horror-struck. "No, Marcus," she protested. "Please . . . you don't understand!"

"*I think I do.*"

With a fury reminiscent of his outburst on their honeymoon, he brushed her denial aside. What did she take him for, anyway? A blind man, or a fool? Wasn't her eagerness to have done with him all too plain in her every look, every gesture?

Letting go of her for a moment, he stabbed viciously at the servants' call button. Within seconds Alistair Simonds appeared.

"On no account is anyone to disturb us here," he informed the butler. "Is that absolutely understood?"

"Yes, sir." His face devoid of expression, Simonds softly closed the door.

"Now, then." Ripping off his tie and starting to unbutton his shirt, Marcus turned back to her. "It may not be part of the bargain," he said, "but I think we should have one more go at things . . . if only in celebration."

Their lovemaking that night, consummated on soft pillows and the drawing room's Turkish carpet, was as fierce and passionate as their encounter on the Breton beach. Marcus took her like a man possessed, driven by anger, sorrow and an overwhelming lust to have her, though this mingling of their bodies should be the last.

Upset though she was, she couldn't refuse him. Unprotesting at first, she came swiftly to life in his arms. Desperately she returned his kisses, helping him strip off the barrier of her clothing and bending her body to his.

"You're mine, Rachel," he groaned as he took her into a maelstrom of longing. "In the most intimate way possible. It's too late now to change that..."

"I don't *want* to change it!" The words were wrung from her, but they came too late. Lost in shudders of completion, he was deaf to any argument. Almost immediately she followed. Tears wet her cheeks as she was racked by a pleasure both sharp and bittersweet.

For a moment they collapsed in each other's arms. Then, as abruptly as he might break off a business deal that had gone sour, Marcus got to his feet. He was overcome with remorse and self-loathing.

Please God, I wouldn't have taken her if she hadn't softened to me that way, he thought. I hope I'm not the kind of man to force himself on the mother of his child.

Yet he was far from certain he stood innocent in that regard. In his heart he believed her response had been a purely physical one, wrested from her at some elemental level against her will.

Another troubling thought occurred as he pulled on his clothes. "I...haven't hurt you, have I?" he asked, fixing her with a keen look. "Tell me the truth."

"No," she whispered.

Burdened by guilt, he couldn't read the message of love and forgiveness in her eyes.

"If I did, I'm sorry," he said, tugging on his shirt though he didn't bother to button it. "I've behaved like a cad . . . a thorough rotter. I bloody well promise you it won't happen again."

Not giving her a chance to answer, Marcus left the room.

Tears blurred her vision as she fumbled for her things. For the sake of their child, she reminded herself, she couldn't afford to become hysterical. A miscarriage was the last thing she wanted.

After Rachel set the room and herself right, she opened the door a crack. There was no one about. Trembling with embarrassment, she darted across the hall and up the oak-and-marble stairs to her bedroom.

What will Simonds think? she wondered, flinging herself across her canopied bed. And the other servants?

But their opinions scarcely mattered beside her husband's. Rachel pictured Marcus shut up in his connecting room, pacing as he brooded. How she longed to go to him, to insist he hear the truth.

A moment later she abandoned the idea. By now she knew Marcus well enough to realize it might be days, even weeks, before he was ready to listen to her.

In the meantime, she suspected, they'd continue to live rigidly separate lives but without the nightly ritual of lovemaking to sustain them. Pulling a comforter over herself, she muffled fresh tears against her pillow.

Rachel came down to breakfast the next morning faintly nauseous and puffy eyed. A cream-colored envelope was propped beside her plate. Barely managing to contain herself until the maid had poured out her coffee and left the room, she tore it open with shaking fingers.

As she'd expected, Marcus's powerful handwriting slashed at the expensive notepaper. "Once again, let me offer my apologies," he'd written in his jagged script. "The last thing I want is to hurt you or our baby. You may be certain you won't have to suffer that kind of indignity again."

A large *M* was scrawled at the bottom of the single sheet.

I've got to set matters straight with him, she anguished, letting her coffee cool. Tell him the truth about how I feel, even if he rejects me for it. With our baby on the way, I can't afford to stand on pride.

Her thoughts were interrupted as Simonds came into the room. "Pardon me, madam, but Mrs. Banks of the Margaret Bowes Center is on the phone," he announced, observing her closely. "Shall I tell her you can't be disturbed?"

"Yes, please. Say I'll ring her back sometime before lunch."

"Very good."

"And Simonds—"

"Yes, madam?"

Rachel hesitated. She didn't like to parade their troubles before the servants, even by placing an unaccustomed call to Marcus at his office. Yet her instincts counseled there was little time to waste.

"Please get me Mr. Davenport."

Expecting raised eyebrows, she hadn't bargained on the butler's thoroughly embarrassed look.

"I'm afraid I can't do that, madam," he said. "It's half past nine already. By now, Mr. Davenport's plane will have taken off for New York."

To Rachel's shock and distress, Marcus had bowed out of her life without actually saying goodbye.

Several weeks passed without either a phone call or a telegram. Their only communication was through Alan Travers, who called frequently to inquire about Rachel's health and to ask if she needed anything. He seemed to know as little as she did about Marcus's projected date of return.

Ironically she heard of her husband almost immediately through Jocelyn Banks. Returning the director's call somewhat later than she'd originally intended, Rachel was met with effusive gratitude over a handsome gift he'd made to the center.

"Thanks to him, curtailed services and make-do facilities are a thing of the past for us," Mrs. Banks said. "Though Mr. Davenport has never set foot in our facility, he's committed a small fortune to its development. Clearly he loves you very much."

I wish you were right, Rachel thought sadly, putting down the phone at the end of their conversation. If so, I'd be the happiest woman in the world. She deeply appreciated Marcus's generosity to a cause so close to her heart, but she saw it as another apology, not as a gesture of affection.

Though time seemed to drag to Rachel, soon she realized that Marcus had been gone a full month. She tried to keep abreast of his travels through Alan Travers, following her husband in imagination as he moved restlessly from New York to his Paris office and back again, with several trips to the Orient sandwiched in between.

During an unscheduled overnight stop he made in London, she was at Depthford House, his estate near Richmond upon Thames, where she'd gone to cheer herself by breathing some fresh country air. If she'd known of his presence in London, she would have gone flying back there in her car. Unfortunately, she didn't learn about it until after his departure, and only then through a secretary's slip of the tongue.

It didn't surprise her when they made the gossip columns again—this time with hints that their marriage was on the rocks. A photo in one of the tabloids pictured Marcus with a slender, sophisticated-looking blonde at a Singapore polo club. To Rachel's chagrin, it was captioned, "Eligible Once

Again?'' Despite his insistence the night he'd proposed marriage that they live their own lives, she was deeply wounded at the thought that someone could take her place.

Poring over the photograph, she noted her husband's uncomfortable frown. His displeasure at having the moment recorded for posterity was all too evident. What does he think I'll do, file for divorce when I see it? she asked herself. He should know better than that. No matter how much our estrangement hurts, I'd never do anything that would mean giving up our baby.

Heartsick but reminding herself she'd known from the beginning what to expect, she tried to remain calm and think of her unborn child. With a vengeance, she buried herself in work at the center and spent long hours in her studio. Despite the unhappy thoughts that flitted through her mind, her watercolors were succeeding beyond her wildest dreams.

A week after Rachel saw the tabloid, Marcus idly picked up a tattered copy of the same newspaper during a brief stopover in Hong Kong. He cursed roundly when he saw the photograph. Downing several stiff drinks in one of the crown colony's most exclusive bars, he canceled dinner plans with the chief of his Orient operations and retreated to the refuge of his hotel.

There, stretched out on his bed with a whiskey and soda, he chain-smoked as he wondered if Rachel would see the shabby little scandal sheet. Maybe she already had.

After the way they'd parted, would she have any reason to guess the blonde clinging to his arm was no *amour* but rather the unscrupulous daughter of one of his business contacts? Or to believe what he knew to be true—that the conniving young woman had set up the photograph, probably in hopes of driving a wedge between Marcus and Rachel?

Rachel doesn't really know or care how rich I am, he realized, letting that surprising yet comforting notion sink deep into his consciousness. Never in a million years would she understand the motivations of a gold digger like Amanda Beale.

It occurred to him that a jealous reaction on Rachel's part might mean she cared for him. For perhaps the thousandth time, he let his mind play over the way she'd shrunk back from him after announcing she was going to have his baby. Had the gesture really signaled her wish to break off their physical relationship, as he'd concluded? Or had his outrageous behavior simply put her off for a moment?

How I wish I could go home, he thought. Just take her in my arms and hold her. Feel the shape of our child growing in her body. We wouldn't have to make love. But he didn't trust himself to stop short of that delirious pleasure. And the press of business was overwhelming.

Not for the first time was he tempted to pick up the phone and call her, instead of going through Alan to find out how she was. But the habit of isolation was too strong. Besides, what would he say to her? He lit another cigarette.

Rachel was four months pregnant and feeling quite lonely when her father stopped in London at the end of his latest European crusade.

"Where's your husband?" he asked bluntly when she reported to his hotel on Grosvenor Square as he'd requested. "You might at least have brought him along."

How like her father to arrange, on his own turf, a possible first meeting with his new son-in-law, she thought. She found herself regarding Luther Vanden's crimped graying hair, arrogantly pugnacious chin and outmoded glasses as if he were a figure from the distant past. His opinions no longer had the power to sway her.

"Marcus is out of the country, Dad, traveling on business," she replied, knowing full well the explanation wouldn't suffice.

"I'm not surprised to hear it." His features taking on their righteous look, Rachel's father let go of the curtain he'd lifted to observe the traffic below. "Don't think for one minute, miss," he said, "that gossip doesn't reach us in America."

When she didn't answer, he let his gaze fall to the gently protruding curve of her abdomen beneath the soft gathers of her silk dress.

"Marcus Davenport's behavior has been well noted," he said in his sermonizing tone. "In our opinion, a husband who would cheat on his wife during her pregnancy doesn't deserve the title. Despite the allure of his wealth, we feel you should come home with us."

He didn't bargain on the fact that she would defend Marcus's reputation.

"It's an insult to me, Dad," she said, "that you'd believe such stories when Marcus and I have been married only a few months. It doesn't sit well, particularly after the way you closed your eyes to Des's infidelity. But of course Des was a generous contributor and close friend—"

"I never condoned Des's behavior!"

For a moment it looked as if Rachel was in for a lengthy diatribe on that subject. Then Luther Vanden softened, and Rachel realized that he'd missed his only daughter.

"Let's not climb down each other's throats during the short time we have together, girl," he urged. "I'm leaving tomorrow for a clerics' meeting in Bath. In fact, I've reserved two rooms at the Royal Crescent Hotel. I was kind of hoping you could join me."

Realizing he was lonely, too, she let her old affection for him surface. "That sounds lovely, Dad," she said, agreeing to go along.

Over dinner the following evening in the Royal Crescent's dining room, Rachel and her father talked quietly of old times, laughing over some of the funny things that had happened. Together they made their first tentative attempts at peace since Rachel had left for London.

In the morning, while her father met with a group of prominent British clerics, Rachel booked an hour in one of the hotel's therapeutic pools. Self-consciously wearing her new maternity swimsuit beneath a street-length terry cover-up, she went downstairs at the appointed hour.

Minutes later she was slipping into warm eucalyptus-scented water beneath a skylit dome. Light filtered through the steamy atmosphere. Flanked by ornate columns, urns and potted palms, the pool made her think of a bath in ancient Rome.

She was quite alone. The attendant switched on a relaxing musical tape and she began to do a lazy sidestroke, parting the gleaming surface of the water with slender graceful hands. Enjoying her buoyancy, she felt almost weightless. She was reminded of her sensuous self for the first time since she and Marcus had made love.

How I miss him! she thought, her physical longing for him suddenly intense. Just the sweet weight of him covering me. The deep feeling of completeness our lovemaking always brings.

Willfully an inner voice reminded Rachel that Marcus probably wouldn't want her when he returned. Already she was noticeably pregnant, her slim waist a thing of the past. Maybe she wouldn't seem sexy or desirable when compared to the glamorous sophisticates of three continents.

Enough of that, Rachel responded. You decided at the outset you'd be strong enough to see things through. Pushing off against the pool's tiled apron, she swam vigorously to the other side.

When her hour was up, she dried off and dressed in a new loose outfit that flattered her changing shape. Pinning up her hair in an Edwardian-style pouf, she lightly applied makeup and asked the doorman to call her a cab. She was due to meet her father for lunch at noon in the Pump Room, a restaurant situated above the town's real Roman baths.

Its bank of windows overlooking a greenish rectangular pool, the Pump Room was the picture of eighteenth-century elegance. Portraits evocative of that era looked down on lunching patrons in modern dress. In one corner a string quartet was playing.

Her footsteps creaked softly on the gleaming wood floor as the maître d' showed her to a pink-and-white napped table. As she'd expected, her father was late. While she waited, sipping ice water from a crystal goblet and surveying the room, she couldn't help overhearing a conversation among three wealthy-looking women at the next table.

To her dismay, they were discussing her and her husband—specifically the "inexplicable mistake" of

Marcus's marriage to her. Referring to several recent gossip items, they finally got around to mentioning that photograph taken in Singapore.

"Cynthia says his new wife's all wrong for him," a cool elegant blonde reported in her upper-crust British accent. "Definitely the ingenue type and a bit of a prude, if you know what I mean."

"They say the poor thing's already pregnant and stuck at home," a brunette rejoined. "What *can* have possessed him to marry an American evangelist's daughter?"

A third woman, who had a kinder face than the others, had been glancing about the room as they spoke. "Shh," she advised her companions. "Dr. Vanden's in town, you know. His daughter may be with him."

Embarrassed, hurt and so angry she didn't trust herself to remain in the restaurant without causing a scene, Rachel abruptly quit her table, but not before hearing the blond woman exclaim softly, "Oh dear, Cecily... I think that was she!"

Leaving a note of apology and explanation for her father, Rachel fled back to the hotel. Quickly she packed her bags and caught the London train.

Safe at home in the Belgravia house, she shut herself up in her room. For several days she ate little and didn't bother to go outside. Stubbornly she refused to take any calls. Her only visitor was her father, who stopped by on his way to the airport to make sure she was all right.

Alan simply showed up at her door late one morning and persuaded her to go out to lunch. He'd been worried when he couldn't reach her by phone, and his company proved to be just the tonic she needed. After extracting a promise he wouldn't tell Marcus, she confessed her ordeal in Bath and was pleasantly surprised when he made light of the women's cattiness.

"You know rumors have a way of getting out of hand," he reminded her over a table at Le Gavroche. "Like mine... Marcus's reputation with women is somewhat overblown."

*"Yours?"* she asked. Forgetting to feel sorry for herself, she tried to picture her husband's assistant as a ladies' man.

Alan rewarded her skepticism with a self-deprecating grin. "See what I mean?" he laughed. "You'd hardly be lunching with the Rake of Fleet Street if you set any store by that kind of gossip—or your reputation!"

As the weeks passed and Marcus still didn't return, she and Alan began regularly lunching together. Gradually they became fast friends. Despite her condition, Rachel guessed that he could easily have learned to care for her. But she was Marcus's wife, and he was too scrupulous to push for anything more than friendship. Quietly admiring, he was simply there for her if she needed him.

I don't know what I'd do without him, Rachel thought, returning home one afternoon from lunch and a delightful walk afterward in Hyde Park. If it weren't for Alan, I'd forget what it's like to be an interesting and attractive woman.

Her connection to the Margaret Bowes center and Jocelyn Banks was another saving grace. Most of the women who worked or volunteered there had already been through pregnancies of their own. She found them willing to answer any questions she might have about childbirth. Their placid assurances more than calmed her fears.

But though she'd reconciled with her father and built a life of sorts for herself, she continued to long for Marcus's love. One day, without warning, he returned. She was standing barefoot before her studio worktable, clad in maternity jeans and an old shirt, and nibbling thoughtfully on the handle of a paintbrush, when she looked up to find him watching her from the doorway.

"Marcus!" she exclaimed.

"The same." He smiled wryly. "You look pleasantly occupied."

Standing there in his creased business suit with shadows under his eyes and strain lines visible about his mouth, he looked incredibly weary. Yet to Rachel he was still the best looking man in the world.

How she longed to run to him!

She stifled the impulse as he appraised her changed physical state. Will he still find me attractive, she wondered, holding herself in suspended animation.

Or will all his excitement be for the signs of our baby's growth?

Had Marcus even guessed at what she was thinking, he'd have enfolded her hungrily in his arms. How lovely she looks, he thought, with that special glow of motherhood about her and her beautiful ripening body, grown heavier with our child. Yet how self-contained she seems. I wonder if she's forgiven me—or missed me at all these past months.

"I must say pregnancy agrees with you, Rachel," he commented when she didn't speak. "Almost six months along and feeling wonderfully well, if Alan is to be believed."

Is he just going to stand there looking at me that way, she wondered? Why doesn't he take me in his arms?

"Actually, yes," she said, giving him a hesitant smile. "The baby moves all the time now. I think he's going to be a restless physical type...like his father."

Her words made Marcus remember the act of conception. His thoughts full of vivid imagery, at first he didn't answer.

"How can you be sure it isn't a girl?" he asked, consciously forcing some of the sexual tension out of his body. "I'd like a daughter every bit as much. Well, let's see what you've been working on."

Their hands brushed as he stood beside her at her worktable, examining and praising her luminous watercolor of two blond working-class children, backlit before a bleak-looking window frame. Rachel thought she would die of the sudden desire she felt. She was overcome, just breathing in his clean, spicy man-scent again and listening to the comforting rumble of his voice.

Somehow she managed to keep her composure as she thanked him for his favorable critique and inquired about his travels.

"I'll tell you all about them at dinner, if you like," he answered. "Tonight, tomorrow and the next day, if it takes that long. I'm scheduled to be at home now for several weeks."

A moment later he kissed her lightly on the cheek and excused himself in the interest of getting some rest.

He's here—in the house! Rachel thought, sinking into a worn peacock chair that had made the trip to Belgravia from her Chelsea flat. I can see him, talk to him, touch him! The idea that, tired as he was, he'd climbed to her third-floor aerie immediately upon his arrival was almost too much to contemplate.

Yet, despite his long absence, there hadn't been any physical demonstration of affection. Just that brief, almost fraternal kiss. I'll have to go slow, she decided. Assume nothing where he's concerned. I'm my own woman now. If he wants me, then he can tell me so. But adamant as she was, her eyes sparkled at the thought.

She was disappointed to find that the Marcus who regaled her at dinner with tales of the glitches in building his new Singapore hotel and hair-raising corporate ventures in America was still moody, though he was in a gentler frame of mind than the one who'd gone storming out of her life.

The days passed and they spent quiet, faintly melancholy evenings in the room where they'd last made love. Several times she imagined he'd like something more intimate from her than companionship, but he made no move in that direction. Kissing each other with polite deference, they went off each night to their separate rooms.

Finally, after she'd given up hope desire would flare between them again, at least during her pregnancy, she was stepping out of her private shower one evening when he walked unannounced into her room. Embarrassed and quite conscious of her condition, she hastily covered herself with a towel.

This time Marcus didn't misinterpret the gesture. He realized she was embarrassed rather than off-putting. Crossing the space between them, he set the towel firmly aside.

"That's my baby, too, Rachel," he said, his voice rough-edged with emotion. "I want to feel it...see what it looks like while it's still in your body."

More gently than she'd have thought possible, he placed one hand on her stomach. Just then the baby kicked as if it recognized its father's touch.

"Do you really mind my seeing you this way?" he asked, his voice a whisper.

Swallowing, she nodded.

"But why?" he persisted. "To me, your body is beautiful."

Her tears slipped out of control at that. "How *can* it be when I'm so big and you—I mean we—don't love each other?"

Slowly Marcus shook his head. "Ah, Rachel," he confessed, betraying a wealth of feeling he kept largely hidden even from himself. "Don't you know I adore you this way?"

# Chapter Ten

Softly murmuring words of praise, he ran his hands over her body. The towel lay pooled like a fallen toga about her feet.

"Let me love you," he begged, reverently caressing her breasts and the opulent curve of her stomach. "I won't hurt you, I promise. I'll treat you like a goddess of heaven and earth."

"Oh, Marcus!" Overcome by his note of supplication, Rachel hid her face against his shoulder.

"Tell me it's all right," he insisted. "I won't take you against your will."

"You wouldn't . . . be doing that."

Sweeping her up into his arms the way he had on their wedding night, he settled her with extravagant care against the piled-up pillows on her bed. In the soft glow from her bedside lamp, she couldn't read his expression. Yet something about his attitude suggested he was steeling himself to depart.

"Say you want me, Rachel," he repeated. "That it's not just willingness on your part to let me have my way. Otherwise . . ."

Tightly her arms clung about his neck. "I *want* you, Marcus," she admitted. "Please don't go."

With a little groan, he freed himself and took off his things. As she lay there looking up at him, Rachel thought he must be the most beautiful man in all the world.

I hope we do have a son, she thought. Our little boy would have eyes like his, and he'd have the incandescent personality that comes through when Marcus throws off the shackles on his emotions.

A moment later there was no need for words. Only the most elemental thoughts possessed her as her husband came to lie beside her and lead her into love.

His kisses were like wine—warm, deep, deliberately intoxicating. Then he moved to her breasts and his mouth tugged with great tenderness yet overwhelming hunger. Cradling his dark head against her, Rachel imagined their child exacting the same privilege. Pleasure knifed through her as she pictured him looking on while she nursed their baby.

Afterward our child will sleep, sated with milk, she thought. Marcus will make love to me and sleep all night in my bed.

Careful of her comfort, he entered her as they lay curled on their sides. Unlike past lovemakings, the one they shared that night was almost motionless. Yet conversely it was one of the most profound.

Depth, possession and release, and a minimum of movement kindled a hot glow that spread in great, compelling ripples through her body. Longing peaked and retreated to peak again with greater intensity. Their union seemed intimately connected to the rhythms of the universe.

Their child made them one already. Now Rachel wanted to grant Marcus her very essence, become an inextricable part of him so that there could be no more separation.

Such thoughts only enhanced the exquisite sensations he was evoking. All too quickly Rachel found herself trembling on the brink of release—reaching with all her being for consummation yet clinging desperately to prolong the moment.

Fused to Marcus, she passed the point of no return. Seconds later the floodgates opened, drowning her in a sea of delight and completion that was like manna to her soul.

Unable to stop himself, Marcus was carried with her on the tide. He shook with his own satisfaction and gooseflesh feathered over his back and shoulders as he buried his face against her hair.

For a long time they lay there, fitted together with the curve of his body sheltering hers, bathed in the contentment of afterglow as their most intense feelings subsided. Then the baby moved again. Marcus caught the faint fluttery sensation.

"I haven't hurt you, have I?" he whispered, resting his palm lightly against her stomach.

"Oh, no." Turning to face him, Rachel kissed his mouth. "If you could only realize what this has meant."

"I know what it's meant to me," he said.

He didn't think there was any way she could guess how much he'd needed her. For one thing, he hadn't given her the slightest indication.

I wish to God I didn't have to leave again, he thought as they shifted positions to prepare for sleep. More than anything, I want to be here with her. Watch our child grow. Make love to her at night.

It was as if Rachel sensed at least one part of his thoughts.

"Stay with me. Stay..." she pleaded, suddenly insecure as she burrowed against him. "Tell me that when I wake up tomorrow, I won't find you gone."

In response he drew her more closely into his arms. "I'm sorry, Rachel," he said, the note of regret very clear in his voice. "But that's what I came to your room to talk about. In the morning, I have to fly out of the country again."

Though she didn't answer, he could feel her tears against his shoulder.

"There's another problem in Singapore," he explained, cursing his responsibilities and knowing she wouldn't understand them. "Plus I have to deal with that expanded tourist agreement with the Soviet government I told you about. The commissars at Intourist expect to negotiate with me personally. I may not like it, but I've a mountain of work to do if I'm to return to London before our baby's birth.''

Still Rachel didn't speak, though she muffled all protest. If he stays away until my confinement, she thought, heavy of heart, that means another three months. I'll be spending Christmas alone.

Yet all wasn't lost, and she knew it as he lightly stroked her hair. Long after she'd given up all hope, he'd come back to make love to her. Tonight he was hers—at least until she fell asleep.

This time, Marcus called her every week or so to inquire about her welfare. On Christmas Eve he phoned from Singapore to say how much he'd hoped he could fly back to London for a few days, until a bout of flu had laid him low. Now that it was too late to make it for the holiday, it made sense to press on with the task at hand, didn't it? That way he'd have more time to spend with her after the baby's birth.

Two weeks later, in mid January, he phoned again. She was almost asleep when a very correct but clearly approving Simonds put through his call.

''How are you, Rachel?'' Marcus asked, his voice sounding as if it came from somewhere beneath the sea, though she knew it was probably being relayed by satellite. ''And the baby?''

Just as he had during an earlier conversation, Marcus had put her first. A glow settled in the region of her heart, and she sent an unspoken message winging to her unborn child—*It's Daddy calling!*—even as she answered him.

"We're both fine," she said, stretching luxuriously under the bed covers. "You might as well know I'm getting big as a house. Do oversize babies run in your family?"

Marcus grinned, and she could sense his expression though she couldn't see it. "Not that I know of," he answered, taking pleasure in her forthright description. Then he frowned. "I hope the little rotter doesn't get too big. I don't want him giving you trouble."

"Dr. Martindale says I'll be just fine. Marcus, I've been thinking...."

The line hummed empty for a moment as he waited.

"If it's a boy, I'd like to call him Jonathan. Sarah if it's a girl."

"Either Jonathan or Sarah will be fine," he said.

He was on the verge of telling her he might wrap up his business early, but he decided against it. There was no sense in getting her hopes up, if indeed his presence mattered that much to her. Problems could come up with the bank buy in New York and he'd just have to cancel.

"Marcus?" she asked, a bit less drowsily though her voice still reminded him of smooth sheets and silky sleep-warmed skin. "Are you still there?"

"I'm still here," he said.

"Where is here?" she asked.

Static interfered, but still she made out his answer. "Moscow," he said. "A hotel off Red Square. I couldn't sleep so I decided to call."

At his request Rachel described her life in his absence. "I spend a lot of time at the center," she said. "And in my studio, of course. I'm more tired these days. But the painting is going well."

In his far-off hotel room, Marcus frowned a little. "You ought to get out more," he said.

Rachel smiled. "Oh, I do. I take walks around the square every afternoon. And Alan's been an angel. He asks me to lunch at least once a week."

His frown deepening, Marcus tried to picture his wife and his trusted assistant dining together at all his favorite luncheon spots. The other patrons in the restaurant they chose had probably assumed that Alan was the father of his baby.

Then he shook off his mood. Rachel wouldn't mention her friendship with Alan so blithely if she had anything to hide.

Changing the subject to his intended route from Russia to Japan, and thence to San Francisco and America's East Coast, Marcus extracted a promise that she take care of herself and the baby. All too soon they were saying goodbye.

Replacing the receiver, Rachel cuddled deeper under the coverlet. She tried to imagine Marcus in his exotic surroundings but got only a fuzzy picture of marching soldiers and Lenin's tomb. Still she was content, almost comfortable, despite her child's nocturnal restlessness. Maybe he doesn't love me— yet, she thought. But there's genuine caring between us. I can feel it. For the moment, I'm willing to settle for having him as a protector and friend.

When the New York bank deal closed ahead of schedule, Marcus was beside himself with delight and anticipation. Never had he wanted so much to return to London or so avidly packed his traveling cases.

Though he customarily slept on transatlantic flights, this time he stayed awake for hours, drinking coffee above the ocean's blackness and thinking of what the future might bring.

Only a month remained now until the birth of their child. How he longed to cuddle that tiny precious life in his arms! And to hold the baby's mother! I'm like a kid, he thought, eager to see how Rachel looks when she's "big as a house." Quite frankly, I glory in the fact that I'm the man who made her that way.

Though he hadn't been present when Jamie was born, he was anxious to share this delivery. Yet all his zeal wasn't for the baby he'd so desperately wanted. A good portion of it is for Rachel, he admitted, picturing her dark-fringed eyes and tender mouth. It'll be hard to wait until my beautiful wife is ready to make love to me again.

By the time Marcus arrived at Heathrow, he'd had only a few hours' sleep. He briefly paused at a pay telephone after clearing customs, then he shook his head, deciding to let his return be a surprise. Buying Rachel a huge bouquet of roses, he headed toward the baggage claim.

At that very moment, Rachel was getting into the Daimler outside their Belgravia residence. Missing Marcus and restless in her very pregnant state, she was on her way to shop for baby things and have tea with Alan.

Sorting through tiny, beautifully made garments at one of the Mayfair area's finest baby shops, Rachel whispered lovingly to her unborn child.

"You can't fool me, Jonathan," she said. "I know you're a boy. And I'm going to prove I have the courage of my convictions, by getting you this adorable sailor suit."

Alan waved to her from the front of the store as she made her final selection. "You're looking healthy as a horse," he teased with the easy familiarity that lay between them. "I say, who were you speaking to just then, back among the blankets and teething rings?"

"Jonathan," she answered with a laugh, gratefully handing him her packages. At his raised eyebrows, she added, "That's what Marcus and I have decided to call the baby if it's a boy. And I'm absolutely certain that'll be the case.''

"I thought we might try Fortnum and Mason today," Alan suggested. "I'll admit I skipped lunch in anticipation of their trifle. It's a calorie-laden delight."

After threading its way through heavier-than-usual traffic from the airport, Marcus's cab was just arriving in Belgrave Square. Roses in hand, he peeled off the fare plus a generous tip and bounded up the steps, leaving the driver to haul in his bags.

"Where *is* she?" he asked Simonds, his dark blue eyes glittering with anticipation. "Upstairs painting, I suppose—"

"I'm afraid madam left nearly an hour ago, sir," the butler answered regretfully. "I don't think she was expecting you. I daresay she wouldn't have gone off, had she known...."

Simonds lapsed into an awkward silence. He had overstepped his bounds and he knew it. But the look of eagerness on his longtime employer's face—replaced by swift, almost searing disappointment—had made him want to set matters straight.

Marcus didn't appear to notice. "Do you know where she went?" he asked, setting the roses on a hall table.

"Shopping, I believe." The butler had partially regained his composure. "And then to tea with Mr. Travers."

So it was *Alan* again. Marcus's frown only deepened. "Any idea where?" he asked.

Simonds strove not to show any undue emotion. "Madam didn't say," he answered. "I expect her back about five o'clock."

Quickly Marcus extracted the information that the Daimler was at his disposal. "If Mrs. Davenport phones, you may tell her I'm out looking for her," he said, bent on taking some kind of action, however fruitless.

Though how I'm going to find her in a city the size of London, he added silently as Jervis held the car door for him, is anybody's guess.

At Fortnum and Mason's mezzanine tearoom, Rachel and Alan shared a marble-topped corner table. Her array of packages from the children's shop reposed on a separate butterfly-patterned metal chair.

True to his word, Alan ordered the trifle, though Rachel turned up her nose at its monstrous calorie-count, opting instead for a modest portion of gooseberry tart.

"I don't want to look like a beach ball when Marcus gets back," she laughed, sipping at her herbal tea. "Any idea when he's expected?"

Alan shrugged. "With the boss, you never can tell."

On their way out, they paused under Fortnum and Mason's famous clock so Alan could buy her a nosegay. Though it was the end of January, the day was breezy and fair. Her pleated cornflower-blue silk maternity dress, revealed by the open front of her white wool coat, blew against her body, outlining the shape of her unborn child.

Their hands innocently brushed as he presented her with a bouquet of bachelor's buttons. Just then, out of the corner of her eye, Rachel saw the Daimler pull up at the curb. Its usual driver was at the wheel.

"I don't understand," she began, giving Alan a puzzled look. "I quite distinctly told Jervis you'd be bringing me home."

Seconds later, to their mutual astonishment, Marcus alighted. By some miracle, he'd spotted them just as he was about to return home in defeat.

Forgetting all else, Rachel ran to him. "Marcus!" she exclaimed. "Darling, why didn't you phone?"

Irked as he was from his restless scouring of fashionable West End districts and the seemingly intimate posture in which he'd found her, the endearment was lost on him. Coldly he looked from her to Alan and back again, and Rachel realized Marcus was jealous of her completely above-board and blameless relationship with Alan. Even his belated greeting was a kind of accusation.

"Hello, Rachel," he said at last. "I need to speak with Alan. But that's no reason for you to discontinue your shopping."

Before she fully understood what was happening, he was ushering her into the Daimler and piling up her packages on the front seat.

"Marcus," she pleaded, rolling down the passenger window. "You've only just returned. Can't your meeting with Alan wait?"

White-faced and comprehending the situation all too well, Alan was about to protest. Marcus silenced him with a look.

"I'm afraid not," he answered, turning back to Rachel. "I'll join you tonight at dinner. That is, if you're available."

At a curt nod from his employer, Jervis pulled out into the stream of traffic. Helplessly Rachel watched the receding figures of her husband and his assistant through the Daimler's rear window.

That evening Marcus was aloof and hostile looking when he appeared at the dinner table.

"We have to talk," Rachel insisted after the first course was served and the maid had retreated. "I can't help but feel that you were upset to return home this afternoon and find me with Alan. But you must realize I'd have waited for you here at home if you'd given me any kind of warning."

It was an unfortunate choice of words.

"I shouldn't think a *warning* would be needed," he responded, putting down his soupspoon. "At least not where a faithful wife is concerned."

How dare he question her fidelity? Anger flared in Rachel's eyes so that their stormy expression matched his. Yet she tried to remain as conciliatory as possible.

"Alan and I are friends and that's all," she countered, her tone suggesting he was a fool to think otherwise. "You yourself assigned him to keep an eye on me. With you gone for months on end, I've been lonely. His companionship has meant a lot."

Marcus regarded her through narrowed eyes. "Alan has flown to New York this evening in my place," he announced. "Meanwhile, I'm back to stay until after the baby's birth. You'll have to derive whatever comfort you can from that."

Thoroughly distraught at his lack of faith in her, Rachel insisted a second time that there was nothing between her and Marcus's very kind, very proper subordinate.

"I'm eight months pregnant, for God's sake," she reminded him. "What man in his right mind would find me attractive in this state?"

The reference to her physical state struck an emotional chord and he softened a little. "I know one who would," he said, stifling the urge to bridge the distance between them.

Upset by the tumult of their argument, Rachel mistook his meaning. "If you mean Alan," she shot back heatedly, "you're wrong! Even if he felt as you say, which I'm sure he doesn't, he'd never breach a trust. As for your doubts about *me*, don't forget we have a bargain. *You've* certainly seen fit to take advantage of that!''

''Have I really?'' Marcus's voice took on a dangerous edge, but he didn't defend himself when Rachel flashed back that even she, despite the sheltered life she led, sometimes read the scandal sheets.

Let her believe a pack of lies about me if that pleases her, he thought furiously. Yet despite her allusion to the marriage agreement he'd exacted, he didn't stop to think he had laid the groundwork for her vulnerability to gossip.

''So?'' he asked, carefully setting his napkin aside. ''What if you do read trash and set store by it? That doesn't change anything. However you feel about me, I'll be staying here, not Alan, to look after you and my baby.''

The conversation ended as he left the room.

Angry, hurt and feeling increasingly ill though she couldn't put her finger on any specific ailment, Rachel tried to eat for the sake of her child. But she could do little more than pick at her food. Giving up, she bypassed the study where she knew Marcus would be smoking, drinking and pacing and went directly up to her room.

I'll just lie down for a little while, she thought, stretching out and pulling the coverlet over herself. She didn't really expect to fall asleep.

The luminous dial of Rachel's bedside clock read a quarter past two when she awoke, still fully dressed in the outfit she'd worn to lunch. For a moment she lay still, not quite certain what had awakened her.

Then suddenly she knew. Clutching at the bed covers, she chronicled the oddly engrossing pain that seemed to rise from her pelvic area to just beneath her breasts. As she waited, hushed, it receded, flowing downward whence it had originated.

Labor pains? she thought warily. But it was a month too early for that. Perhaps she shouldn't have tried to eat when she was so upset.

When nothing else happened for several minutes, she threw off her quilt and got up to change into a nightgown. She had just pulled a full flower-sprigged cotton shift over her head when the pain struck again, stronger this time. Its intensity caused her to grasp hold of the edge of her dresser.

Seconds later a whoosh of clear fluid slipped down her legs. Not moving, Rachel stared fixedly at the damp spot on the carpet. Finally the pain relaxed its hold, and she could move again.

Panicking a little because it was too soon, she stumbled into Marcus's room. His dark head lay motionless on the pillow. Deep and even, his breathing indicated that he was fast asleep.

"Marcus, wake up!" she cried, bending over him and shaking him by the shoulder. "Please, I need you! I think the baby's about to come!"

He was awake in an instant. "Rachel, sweetheart, sit down," he urged, sitting up and putting one arm around her. "Tell me what you're feeling. Are you in any pain?"

As cogently as she could, she described what had happened. "I woke up with this huge cramp that seemed to rise and fall like a wave," she said. "It hurt terribly and yet, in a funny way, it didn't. A few seconds later it was gone. Then it came again. I ... think my water broke ..."

"We've got to get you to a hospital!"

Pressing the servants' buzzer, Marcus managed to pull on a pair of trousers by the time a sleepy Simonds appeared in his bathrobe.

"Have Jervis bring the Daimler around," he ordered distractedly. "As soon as possible. Mrs. Davenport is about to have her baby."

His eyes widening, the butler hurried off to do his employer's bidding.

Marcus had put on a shirt and begun to button it when another labor pain struck. "Hold fast to me, Rachel," he urged, sitting back down on the bed beside her. "Let me be your refuge."

Leaning against him, Rachel let the spasm take her, accommodating her breathing to it and remaining absolutely still until it had passed.

"They're awfully strong and close together, aren't they?" she asked in a worried voice. "I didn't think they were supposed to start out that way."

Helplessly Marcus shook his head. "I don't know, sweetheart," he said. "Hold tight. I'm going to get your coat."

With her feet thrust into bedroom slippers and her white coat covering her nightgown, Rachel made it down the stairs with Marcus's assistance before another pain struck. Each time one hit, she felt lifted out of herself. It was as if a majestic elemental process had claimed her body. Her function was simply to catch the rhythm and cooperate.

When the pain eased, Marcus helped her into the car and got in beside her. "St. Elizabeth's," he barked to Jervis as he put one arm around her. "Don't spare the horses."

Marcus stroked her hair with gentle fingers as they shot out of Belgrave Square and onto one of the city's brightly lit thoroughfares.

"It's going to be all right," he promised. "You'll be fine and the baby will be beautiful. Simonds called the doctor and he'll be meeting us there."

It seemed only a few minutes before they were screeching to a halt outside the hospital's emergency entrance. Blinking in the harsh light, Rachel gasped as another pain engulfed her. Until it was over, she refused to let go of Marcus or get out of the car.

Somebody brought up a wheelchair. "Don't leave me," she begged, reaching for her husband's hand as an attendant helped her into the device and started to wheel her inside. "Please, I don't want to go through this alone."

"You won't."

Firmly he laced his fingers through hers. Apprehensive, her face bare of makeup and wincing whenever a pain struck, Rachel was the most beautiful and special woman he'd ever known. He longed to protect her, nurture her, bear her pain in his own body. If anything should happen to her as a result of his greed for a baby, he thought, he'd never forgive himself.

"Don't worry, my darling wife," he whispered, keeping calm for her sake as they got into the elevator. "I'll be with you every step of the way."

## Chapter Eleven

Outside the labor room Marcus encountered some resistance. A heavyset middle-aged nurse refused to let him come inside, much less scrub and put on a sterile gown to accompany Rachel into the delivery room.

"It's against hospital policy," she intoned, crossing hefty arms over her breasts. "If you have any questions, Mr. Davenport, you're free to call the hospital administrator."

Naturally that official wouldn't be available until morning. Easing out of another pain, Rachel gave Marcus an anxious look.

"I don't give a damn for your policy," he told the nurse, giving Rachel's hand a squeeze. "Perhaps you've forgotten that this floor is known as the

James M. Davenport Maternity Pavilion. I happen to be the donor who paid for its construction, to the tune of several million pounds. As for your administrator, I suggest *you* call him.''

With a shocked look on her face, the woman stepped aside.

That night, as he wiped beads of sweat from Rachel's forehead and encouraged her to dig her nails into his arm, Marcus was the ideal husband. Soothing and comforting, he managed to ease most of her fears.

When she was pronounced ready for delivery, he disappeared for a second and returned in green scrub attire with a mask over his nose and mouth. With the doctor's permission, he stood behind her in the white-tiled delivery room, smoothing her brow and trying to cushion some of her labor.

Inevitably he thought of the way he'd treated her the day before, voicing unfounded suspicions and losing his temper over a situation that was probably his own fault. I swear to God I won't do that again, he thought. From now on, I'm going to cherish her — and our child.

Their eyes met in the overhead mirror as the first signs of the baby appeared. The pains were big now, huge and encompassing the totality of Rachel's being. Yet she knew her ordeal was nearly over. Soon she would hold in her arms the baby she'd wanted so desperately.

Every muscle in his body tensing, Marcus watched her push the slippery red boy-child out into the world. *My son!* he thought, remembering Jamie and wishing his first child could have lived to meet his little brother. But though he'd always love his first-born and preserve the memory of him in his heart, already this child had made a place of his own.

For a moment the baby gasped, traumatized by his journey through the birth canal. Then, as great gulps of air entered his lungs, he set up a tremendous wail, filling the delivery room with a quavery, outraged and thoroughly healthy newborn sound.

"Jonathan," Rachel whispered, her body going limp as the doctor held the baby up for them to see. "I knew all along it was you."

Marcus was wiping away tears. "Ah, sweetheart, he's so beautiful," he said, choking on the words.

Washed, weighed and wrapped in a blanket, Jonathan Marcus Davenport was pronounced whole and vigorous, a hefty seven and a half pounds despite his early arrival. At the age of eight minutes, he was placed in his father's arms.

Cradling his infant son, Marcus let the tears flow unchecked. "How I love him already," he said to Rachel.

"I know," she answered softly. She was thinking how much she loved them both.

Some time later, Marcus visited Rachel and Jonathan in their private room. He was subdued, not jubilant as she'd expected. Bending over to kiss her cheek, he offered her a small bouquet of flowers resembling those which had grown in their meadow along the Breton coast.

Rachel slipped her hand into his, her own heart overflowing with happiness at the presence of baby Jonathan in his bassinet beside her. As she thanked him for the bouquet, she couldn't help but feel it was the gesture of a lover, not just a man who was grateful at being presented with an heir.

"Don't you know," he said, his eyes filled with unprecedented emotion, "that I want to give you both the earth?"

Her heart full, she couldn't answer. Lightly he reached out to stroke Jonathan's soft fuzz of dark hair and offer one tiny fist a finger to clasp.

"From the baby's size," he added, "I can't help but think he was conceived in France, somewhat earlier than we realized. Maybe even on the beach, the way I said then."

Rachel nodded. "I prefer to think it happened in the meadow," she replied gently. "Or the haystack. Or even on our wedding night. But I don't doubt for a moment that you're right."

Overcome by the memory of that stormy afternoon, Marcus pulled up a chair.

As they talked quietly, Rachel began to feel something was bothering him. "What's wrong?" she asked at last. "It's as if there's a small sad edge on your happiness."

As usual he made light of his emotions.

"I didn't guess that day, when he was conceived, that he'd make you suffer so much," he admitted with a little shake of his head. "You see, I wasn't present at my first son's birth."

Eager to comfort him, Rachel slipped her arms around his neck. "Don't think of that now," she urged. "The joy of having him far outweighs the pain."

Marcus continued to hold her for a moment. But it was a long time since they'd been intimate, and after his behavior the day before he felt awkward, almost unworthy of the physical contact.

"I'd better go," he said finally, easing her back against the pillows. "Neither of us has had very much sleep. You and the baby should get some rest."

Left alone with her newborn son, Rachel turned on her side to look at him with love. The child was part of her and part of Marcus, yet he was his own inimitable separate self as he stirred under the blue blanket. He was the dream of a lifetime. At last that dream had come true.

How beautiful you are, baby Jonathan, she thought, examining his delicate, shell-like ears and the tiny fingers that fluttered each time someone entered the room. And how I love you! Already something deep inside her had bonded fiercely with his small precious body. She knew she'd give up her life for him in an instant if it ever came to that.

* * *

The following morning three dozen pink roses arrived along with a congratulatory wire from Alan. "Knew you could do it, old girl," the telegram read in his usual teasing banter. "God bless both you and the baby."

Though she appreciated the gesture and felt real fondness for her husband's assistant, in Rachel's eyes his tribute couldn't compare with Marcus's small bouquet of flowers. Yet when he saw the roses, Marcus's face tightened. Her offer to let him read the wire met with a shake of his head.

I'm not jealous now, he thought, not in the way she thinks I am. But all the moments Alan shared with her during her pregnancy are forever lost to me. Somehow I should have arranged to come back to England more often.

Marcus only felt worse realizing that pride and stubbornness, not true necessity, had prevented that.

This time Rachel didn't hasten to reassure him. Right now, she thought, Jonathan's my first priority. Besides, motherhood had changed her, made her more her own person. She wanted Marcus to appreciate that and meet her halfway. If you want me and the right to be jealous, she thought, then *say* so. You should know I'm already yours.

Marcus lapsed into silence as Rachel undid the bodice of her gown to nurse the baby.

Covertly assessing his expression as he watched Jonathan nuzzle at her breast, she began to hope his disquiet stemmed from something more profound than male territorial defensiveness or remembered hurt at his first wife's betrayal. Somehow, the hunger and deep protective urge she read in his eyes augured a strong emotional attachment both to herself and their baby.

Cuddling her sweet talcum-scented son, she thought how much she'd like Marcus to come and sit beside her on the bed, shelter both of them in his arms. I'd want him to hold us that way forever, she thought. Never to let us go.

Like Marcus, she had her pride. Words of love left unspoken and his absence during most of her pregnancy had created an emotional deficit she couldn't overcome. The gossip columns, with their tongue-in-cheek references to his supposed infidelities, had genuinely hurt. Willing to put the past behind them, no matter what it contained, she felt he should make the first move. Perhaps Jonathan and their mutual love for him would bring them together.

When it was time for them to come home from the hospital, Marcus picked them up in the Jaguar. Rachel proudly dressed her son for his first outing in the miniature blue-and-white sailor suit she'd purchased just a few days before. How long ago that seems now, she thought, easing his arms into the sleeves of a fleecy bunting. And how much has changed!

One of the differences involved her figure. At her request, a maid had sent over a slim gray silk chemise she'd worn during the early days of her pregnancy. With its loose yet slender fit, it hinted at her returning waistline and hid the slight roundness of her stomach.

Plus it has the advantage of buttoning down the front, she thought, surveying herself in her hospital-room mirror. Jonathan will have easy access. She wondered if Marcus would notice the new fullness of her breasts.

Though Marcus was keenly aware of the changes childbirth had wrought in her, he didn't mention them. I don't even want to *think* of making love to her until she's fully recovered, he told himself, helping her on with her coat. Sadly he didn't know any other way to express his feelings.

A pretty young nurse helped Rachel into a wheelchair and deposited Jonathan, cozy in a knit cap and several layers of blankets, on her lap for the trip downstairs. Marcus followed after them, carrying her things.

As he'd warned on his arrival in their room that morning, the weather had shifted. Jonathan's first glimpse of London was of bundled-up pedestrians and surly skies. Driving home, safe in his miniature car seat between his parents, he didn't seem to mind.

Rounding the Victoria and Albert Museum and turning northeast onto Brompton Road, Marcus grinned down at his son. The sheer happiness that flowed from Jonathan's existence was helping ease some of the alienation he'd brought on himself.

"You don't realize it yet, little man," he said, reaching over to tickle the baby gently under his chin, "but this city is going to be your oyster. If your father has anything to say about it, you shall have the best of everything."

After Rachel had finished nursing Jonathan that night and begun to prepare for bed, Marcus knocked lightly and entered her room. "I want to ask you a favor," he said.

Holding her hairbrush in abeyance, she gave him a questioning look.

"I'd like to sleep here with you," he said. "In your bed."

At her look of surprise, he hastened to explain. "I hope you know I'm not cad enough to touch you so soon after you've given birth," he said. "I just want to feel our baby near. Listen to his breathing and little whimpering sounds."

Rachel's heart went out to her dark-haired husband. He's afraid something will happen to Jonathan the way it did to Jamie, she realized. And I can't really blame him. Confident as I am there's no danger of that, I might feel as he does if I'd ever lost a child.

Because of the emotional barriers between them, she knew sharing a bed with him might prove difficult. Yet she wanted to be near Marcus as much as he wanted to be near their baby.

"All right," she conceded, wielding her brush with renewed vigor. "But I warn you you're not likely to get very much rest."

Going to sleep with Marcus beside her yet not touching her in the act of love was easier than she'd expected. Attuned to the rhythms of her baby, her body knew she needed rest. Unlike the night they'd slept together at the Nevilles', she drifted quickly into dreams.

Shortly after midnight she awoke to nurse Jonathan while Marcus, who'd been sleeping in fits and starts, watched. She saw his mixed emotions play over his face. He didn't wake a second time when, around four in the morning, she opened her eyes to the baby's restless stirring.

To Rachel's amazement, she and Marcus had nestled in each other's arms. It was a telling revelation, one she would think about often as she puzzled over their relationship. Nevertheless she wasn't surprised to reawaken later and find him gone.

Several weeks went by and they were still at the same impasse. Marcus continued to share her bed though he scrupulously avoided any hint of physical contact. It was scant comfort to realize, from inadvertent clues he dropped, that their celibate arrangement was just as difficult for him.

Though he worked long hours, going so far as to spend a good part of each evening on the phone with subordinates in various time zones, he didn't mention going out of town again. Despite the business sacrifices involved, he seemed determined to remain in London, watching his son grow and change.

Jonathan was nearly a month old when Rachel received an unexpected invitation.

"I got a telegram today from Joanna McBride, a cousin on my mother's side," she informed Marcus that night at the dinner table. "She was one of my few close friends during high school."

"What was it about?" he asked absently.

He was thinking how lovely his wife looked in her rose-colored silk dress and that heavy single strand of pearls. Though still slender she was lush in a new way, and her figure was even more tempting than the first night they'd made love. The glow she acquired during pregnancy has only deepened, he thought.

"She and several of her women friends will be vacationing in the south of France next week," Rachel answered.

"Oh?" he said.

After a brief pause she continued. "The trip was planned on the spur of the moment. Joanna wants me to join them, at least for a few days. It would be our first chance to get together outside a formal family gathering in years."

Marcus greeted the news with a frown. "I don't see how you can do that, with Jonathan nursing."

"I plan to take him with me," she said.

At that he put down his fork.

On receiving the telegram, Rachel's first reaction had been similar to her husband's. Traveling with the baby hadn't occurred to her at first.

Gradually, though, the idea of seeing Joanna again and soaking up some of the Mediterranean sun had asserted its appeal. In addition she was feeling restless. Her physical desire for Marcus had returned full force, and she was exhausted from the emotional tension between them.

Maybe it *would* be a good idea to go, she'd thought, rereading the telegram as she rocked Jonathan in the morning room. Marcus may appreciate me more if I'm gone for a change. In many ways, a break might help.

But she knew what he'd say when she broached the subject. Ever since Jonathan was born, he'd had a security man at the house in what she considered a gross overreaction to his tragic past.

Watching him now as he stared at her across the dinner table and bracing herself for his objections, she knew he'd fight her. She didn't plan to give in.

"Of course you're free to go if you wish," he said at last, with all the care of a man picking his way through a mine field. "But I don't want you taking Jonathan out of the country. Is this trip worth weaning him to a bottle when you'll be gone just a few days?"

"I have no intention of weaning our baby."

"Then, I don't see how..." he began.

Something about the set of Rachel's mouth warned Marcus he had a battle on his hands. "I expect to go *and* to take him with me," she said. "Despite what you may think, I have no intention of trying to escape either you or our custody arrangement."

He frowned, genuinely surprised at that. "Is that what you think is worrying me?" he asked. "Well, you're wrong. I know you're far too honorable to renege on our bargain. No, it's a different sort of kidnapping I'm afraid of, my innocent. I'm a far wealthier man than you seem to realize, and that makes your sweet baby the target of evil designs."

Careful not to make light of his fears, Rachel persisted. "You're not living up to your guarantee of mutual freedom," she said. "Keeping Jonathan here is tantamount to forcing *me* to remain. I can hardly leave for France without our son when I'm the sole source of his nourishment. And I refuse to stop nursing him simply to allay your fears."

Sensing she was adamant, Marcus gave way finally with extreme reluctance. "I won't oppose your plan," he said, "though I don't like it, provided you take Jonathan's bodyguard with you and stay for just a few days."

"I think that could be arranged." Stunned at her victory, she tried not to show her surprise.

"Of course you'll use the company plane, with my personal pilot at the controls," he added, taking charge of details as if he hadn't just lost the argument. "I'll meet you in Paris on your way home. It turns out I have business there. Besides, I've noticed you're even slimmer than you were before your pregnancy, though your curves are more pronounced. I'd like to buy you some new things."

Putting them on the plane and warning his pilot, Jeb Flannery, not to take any chances, Marcus seemed about to enfold Rachel in his arms. Instead, after kissing their son, he bid her a brusque goodbye and ordered her to "watch out for the both of you." Observing from the window as Jonathan's bodyguard boarded, she saw the man get a similar lecture.

Joanna and her two office mates from the Chicago insurance company where she worked met them at the Nice airport. After hugs, kisses and exclamations over the baby, they insisted Rachel and Jonathan crowd into their rental car for the trip back to their Menton hotel. Jeb Flannery and the bodyguard, Al Munson, followed in an Air Anglia company car. Through Marcus's office, a separate hotel room had been reserved for the two men.

The hotel called Les Colombieres was set in rambling terraced gardens above the city and had only six rooms. With Rachel and the baby occupying a third room, their party took up half the hotel. The view, a vast panorama of tile-roofed houses and azure Mediterranean coves that stretched from Monaco to the Italian border, was positively breathtaking.

How I'd love to be here with Marcus, Rachel thought, throwing open the window of her high-ceilinged frescoed room. Still, the time away from him will serve its purpose.

She felt positively mercenary as she looked forward to lazy hours on Les Colombieres' bougainvillea-draped terrace, caring for her child and soaking up some winter sun. Toiling away in London's fog and damp, Marcus was sure to miss them.

During her stay, Rachel discovered, to her delight, what it was like to be a young girl at a slumber party, an experience she'd missed. She enjoyed sharing a cabana with her cousin and friends one afternoon on Menton's gravelly beach, though she didn't venture into the cool aquamarine-and-turquoise-shaded water.

Their little caravan of rental car and company vehicle also ventured up into the hills, to Tourette-sur-Loup, one of the fortified "perched" villages so typical of that coast. When she returned that night, exhausted from toting Jonathan in his canvas baby carrier, she knew the exertion had been worth it. Someday when she told her son about his first trip abroad, she'd describe the gorge along the river, the scent of herbs growing wild in the valleys, ancient stone and stucco dwellings clinging precariously to the cliffs.

In the evenings they dined out at modest out-of-the-way restaurants, escorted by the handsome pilot and middle-aged bodyguard. Laughing and talking, they sipped the iridescent rosé wine of Provence over grilled fish, ratatouille or *soupe au pistou* and fragrant crusty bread.

Jeb Flannery joined Joanna and her friends when they went nightclubbing, but Al Munson had to remain at the hotel with Rachel and Jonathan. *Boîtes de nuit* were certainly no place for a baby, and Rachel needed some time by herself.

She spent those evenings quietly on the terrace outside her window, well within earshot of Jonathan's slightest sound or movement. Looking at the bay, skimmed by its fairy-tale necklaces of lights, she thought of her relationship with Marcus and pondered her next move.

Since her arrival in Menton, he'd phoned every day, checking on Jonathan and inquiring about her own welfare. Even her cousin had remarked several times about his devotion.

Smiling, Rachel hadn't contradicted Joanna. It's possible she's right, she thought. Maybe he has learned to love me but simply doesn't know how to show it. Yet if that's true, why hasn't he asked to make love to me again?

One thing was certain: she loved him very much. While her stay in Menton had provided much-needed relief from the tensions of physical proximity and emotional distance, she would soon be back in the middle of that situation. Sitting there on her calm moonlit terrace, Rachel knew she couldn't bear for the standoff between them to continue week after week.

There's only one thing to do, she decided, though I may get a humiliating rejection. I must tell him how I feel and offer to have him on any terms.

Eager to face her husband, Rachel was oddly apprehensive as she, Jonathan and Al Munson boarded Marcus's private jet for the flight from Nice to Paris. Perhaps her uneasiness stemmed from the fact that they would be leaving Jeb Flannery behind in a French hospital. He'd been admitted for an emergency appendectomy the night before.

Reason argued there was nothing to worry about. A substitute pilot, a Frenchman who regularly flew commercial jets for Air Anglia, had been found. The company agent in Nice had assured her he would do a first-rate job.

Like Jonathan, Rachel found herself dozing during the uneventful flight. It was only after they were well into their descent to Paris, a bare thousand feet in altitude and about two miles from the airport, that her premonitions were realized.

Suddenly there was a jolting thud, as if something had smashed into the airplane. Its starboard engine began to vibrate wildly, sending such strong tremors through the cabin that Rachel thought it might be pulled apart.

"Jonathan!" she cried.

*"Mon Dieu, ce sont des oiseaux!"* the pilot exclaimed over the open intercom. My God, it's birds! Rachel translated.

Terrified, she snatched up the baby from his portable bassinet at her feet and clutched him to her breast.

As the pilot shut down the ailing engine so that its gyrations wouldn't destroy the plane, they veered alarmingly to port. A moment later he kicked in some extra rudder in an attempt to right them, widely overcompensating. From the window beside her seat, Rachel could see the port engine had been hit, too. It was starting to smoke.

"Prepare for emergency landing!" the pilot shouted in English, switching back to French as he radioed the Roissy tower for crash equipment to meet them on the runway.

Jonathan and I are going to die, Rachel thought, her mind as calm as the eye of a hurricane. We'll never see Marcus again.

Then she remembered that babies sometimes survive air crashes when adults do not. Ready to give up her life for her infant son, she prayed he would make it.

"Goodbye, sweet baby," she whispered, her heart breaking with love as she bent over to shield him with her body. "Don't forget you were the most wanted little boy in all the world."

# Chapter Twelve

Marcus had been waiting eagerly at Air Anglia Operations for the plane to land. Through a speaker that broadcast radio communications between the Roissy tower and his company's aircraft, he'd heard the pilot identify himself and request clearance.

Where's Jeb? he'd asked himself, frowning uneasily. Something must be wrong if he's not at the controls. Strolling over to a wide bank of windows that overlooked the runway, he'd scanned the low-hanging clouds for some sign of the plane, but he'd realized it was too early yet.

Impatiently he'd lit a cigarette. During Rachel's absence, there'd been plenty of time to think—long days and nights in which he'd missed her soft voice and radiant smile, the faint lily of the valley perfume that trailed after her, whispering of silky skin and innocence. Most of all he'd missed the light of love in her eyes as she'd cuddled his dark-haired baby boy against her breast. Fervently he'd wished that love included him.

For too long, he knew, foolish pride had stood in the way of loving her. Even after he'd admitted the truth to himself during lonely nights in Moscow, Singapore and New York and again the night of Jonathan's birth, that same cursed pride had prevented him from saying what he felt.

*Once she's back in my arms,* he vowed, preparing to walk downstairs and meet her, *I won't let her go until we settle things. If I have my way, we won't waste any more time saving face. We'll be too busy making love.*

He was startled from his reverie as the unfamiliar pilot's voice came over the loudspeaker again to request the crash details.

Fear gripped Marcus like a big hand. *My God!* he thought, going cold all over as a thousand thoughts rushed through his mind. *I'm going to lose them. I'll never see Rachel or Jonathan again.*

A technician turned to him, shock and sympathy on his face. "Monsieur Davenport..."

Somehow he answered the man, translating his thoughts into French without stopping to consider it. "I'm going out there!" he exclaimed, unaware he was shouting. "Get me a car...a Jeep...anything!"

\*   \*   \*

"'Ere, Mrs. Davenport, fasten on 'is carrying sling. 'E'll be safer that way.''

The cockney voice at Rachel's elbow belonged to Al Munson. Rapidly and efficiently, the bodyguard slipped Jonathan into his canvas baby carrier and strapped the device on backward so that the baby was facing her body and cushioned tightly against her breast.

"Now, bend over," he instructed. "Put your 'ead between your knees."

The precaution came not a moment too soon. With a shuddering impact, the plane hit the runway. Al Munson was knocked backward into the aisle, striking his forehead on one of the seats. Still wearing her seat belt, Rachel hunched forward to protect her baby.

For what seemed an eternity they hurtled forward, careening wildly as the pilot tried to halt them. Rachel could hear fire trucks screaming alongside as they approached the end-of-the-runway barricade. They briefly skidded sideways, coming to rest, eerily motionless on the edge of the pavement.

Before she realized what was happening, Al Munson was hauling himself to an erect position beside her seat. Blood was streaming from a cut above his eye, and he was holding one arm at an awkward angle, as if it might be broken. Yet he definitely had his wits about him. "Quick," he urged, breaking open her seat belt and pulling her to her feet. "We've got to get off 'er in case she burns."

Already flames were licking at the port engine. Later Rachel would wonder how, with a concussion and several broken bones, the bodyguard was able to wrest open a hatch and help them scramble down a hastily positioned emergency ladder.

Half running, half limping, he dragged them away from the plane as the pilot hit the ground running, motioning frantically for them to get clear. Somehow Rachel managed the flight in her high-heeled pumps without breaking an ankle or pitching forward with Jonathan in her arms.

Gasping for breath, they halted at a safe distance from the crippled aircraft as fire engines surrounded it, spurting huge arcs of chemical foam into the air. Against Rachel's breast, Jonathan was whimpering.

"You're safe, my love," she crooned, loosening the carrying sling so he'd have room to breathe. "Precious baby, everything's going to be all right."

Just then, a Jeep screeched to a halt on the tarmac, followed by an ambulance. There was the sound of running feet.

Seconds later Marcus enfolded them. With a groan he rocked them back and forth as if keening over what he'd almost lost.

Still in shock, Rachel let him hold her. She could feel the wild beating of his heart, sense the surge of relief that coursed through his body. In that moment, she knew they were flesh of his flesh and bone of his bone, herself as much as Jonathan. Oh, Marcus, she thought, wondering if he'd withdraw again later, to build another wall between them. I love you so much.

Somebody yelled that the fire was out. Beside them, paramedics were easing Al Munson onto a stretcher. Wind whipping at their hair and faces, Marcus and Rachel drew back to look at each other.

"It wasn't kidnappers or terrorists, after all. It was birds," she whispered, amazed that they were all right, and stunned by the irony of the situation.

Shaking his head, Marcus drew her close. Softly murmuring endearments, he kissed her hair, her eyes, her mouth, pausing to bury his face against the baby's velvety cheek.

Television cameras were grinding away as emergency workers approached Marcus and Rachel to check on her and the baby. As if on cue, Jonathan, who'd slept through most of the terrifying experience, started to cry.

Letting go of them for a moment, Marcus went over to clasp the bodyguard's uninjured hand. His voice breaking, he thanked the man from the bottom of his heart.

"If it weren't for you, no telling what would have happened to them," he said. "Please, let me know if you lack for anything...no matter what the cost."

Al Munson gave him a lopsided grin. "I'll be all right, Mr. Davenport," he said. "Just take good care of the missus and her little 'un until I get out of 'ospital.''

Together they waited until he was put safely on board an ambulance. "C'mon," Marcus told Rachel, elbowing aside a reporter who tried to shove a microphone into her face. "I'm taking you home."

At the Air Anglia building, they transferred to a chauffeur-driven limousine. Stepping inside his company's headquarters to inquire about the pilot's status, Marcus returned carrying Rachel's sable jacket, purse and luggage from the plane.

"Somebody retrieved these things," he explained, handing them into the car and getting in beside her. Seconds later he was issuing his instructions to the driver. "Paris," he requested in French. "All haste. My—correction—*our* apartment."

As the big car rounded the terminal and headed toward the city, Marcus slipped one arm around her. "I thought I'd lost you and our son," he said, the rough note back in his voice.

Amazed that he'd put her first, she didn't know how to answer him. Meanwhile Jonathan was crying as if his heart would break.

Shrugging open her suit jacket, Rachel unbuttoned her pleated silk blouse. "He's starving and I'm aching for him," she said, cuddling the hungry child against her body.

For a moment Marcus watched, his gaze fixed on her lush breast and soft pink nipple, the child's hungry, seeking mouth. Then, as Jonathan began to nurse, he reached out to smooth the baby's temple, the back of his hand just grazing her skin.

"It would have killed me if I *had*, you know," he added, his beautiful eyes suddenly a window to his tangled emotions. "We have to talk, Rachel ... as soon as we get home and put our son to bed."

By the time they reached Marcus's elegant apartment, Jonathan was sated and ready for sleep. As Rachel held him in her arms and Marcus operated the old-fashioned cage elevator, she felt strongly that they were a family in a very real sense.

Only time will tell if I'm right, she thought. But perhaps the talk Marcus had said he wanted would offer some insight. With the unshakable calm of one who has just faced disaster and come away from it whole, she greeted his elderly French butler and went directly to the Louis Seize master bedroom to put her son to bed.

Tucking Jonathan into his crib, she kissed him good-night. Meanwhile the butler was carrying in her cases. A maid arrived to unpack.

As if she were a figure in a slow-motion film, Rachel bathed and changed into ivory satin lounging pajamas and a matching robe that emphasized her trim yet curvaceous figure. Sitting down before an ornate mirror, she brushed her hair with languid, almost majestic strokes.

Funny, she thought, how this place seems like home to me now, when before I felt so transient. What Marcus told the driver was right.

She turned her head as the maid returned to inform her in perfect English that Monsieur Davenport was waiting for her in the study.

"He says not to hurry, madame," she added, smiling at the baby who was sleeping on his stomach, his little behind humped up under the blanket. "But I think he is anxious to speak with you, all the same."

Rachel returned the woman's friendliness with a smile of her own. "Please tell him I'll be with him in a moment."

Someone had kindled a fire in the study hearth. Marcus, who had been on the phone, put down the receiver when she entered.

"Here, sweetheart, sit down," he urged, taking her by the arm and leading her to a comfortable overstuffed couch that complemented the room's masculine furnishings. "Relax while I fix us each a drink."

Rachel curled up among some pillows. "I believe I'll pass," she said. "It's not such a good idea, you know, to indulge in alcohol when you're nursing a baby."

To her surprise Marcus insisted she partake. "One Scotch won't hurt either you or our son, after all you've been through," he said. "You seem quite calm now. But what happened today is bound to have its impact.''

Agreeing in order to please him, she watched quietly as he plucked ice from a container with silver tongs, dropped it into cut-crystal glasses and poured a jigger of pale amber liquid into each.

What a beautiful man he is, she thought. Deft and economical of motion. How full of fun he can be sometimes, how passionate. Suddenly pensive, she stared into the fire as she replayed the afternoon's events in her mind.

Accepting her glass as he came to sit beside her, she met Marcus's eyes. ''We could have lost everything today,'' she whispered.

Somberly he nodded. ''We're very lucky, my love. We have our son... and, if you want it, another chance to build something very special together.''

Stunned, Rachel took a sip of her drink. Its fiery liquid burned her throat. He had called her his love, and yet, far from retreating, he was leaning forward, resting one hand lightly on her knee. Though she could hardly believe it, there was something dangerously close to love in his deep blue eyes.

''I'm not sure what you mean,'' she told him.

Marcus's voice was husky with emotion. ''If you're willing, I'd like to renegotiate our agreement,'' he said. ''I know it wasn't part of the bargain, but I love you more than life. To my eternal regret, I've behaved like a fool... given you absolutely no reason to return my affection.

"All I ask now is that you reconsider letting me be your husband in every sense of the word. If you agree, I promise to show you in all possible ways just how much you're loved."

Overcome with emotion, Rachel couldn't answer him, though she covered his hand with hers.

"I'd already decided, you know," he added, "even before your plane got in trouble, that this was what I wanted. Hell, I should have realized long ago that I didn't want anybody but you."

It was a long speech, one straight from the heart. And, perhaps for the first time ever, that heart was on his sleeve.

"Marcus," she began, almost tongue-tied as she tried to respond. "If only—"

Watching her, he was suddenly afraid she might refuse. "Don't answer yet," he said, panicking a little. "There's one more thing I have to tell you."

If only you knew how much I've loved you from the beginning, she'd been about to tell him. But perhaps the moment wasn't right for it yet. Quietly Rachel waited for him to speak.

"I want you to know the truth about the gossip you must have heard," he said, making her panic in turn. "And that photograph of me in Singapore, with a voluptuous blonde on my arm. None of it signified anything. Amanda Beale is the daughter of one of my business colleagues, and she set up that photograph for her own very nefarious purposes.

"As for the rumors, that's all they've been. There hasn't been anyone but you in my life, dearest Rachel, since I first made love to you."

Abruptly burdened with more happiness than she'd ever expected would be her lot, Rachel set her Scotch aside on a leather-topped table. In the very depth of her being, she knew she could believe him. Yet she felt greedy now, strong enough to demand everything he had to give.

"If you mean that, Marcus," she said gently, causing him to hold his breath, "then there's something I want you to promise me."

His brows lifted a little. "Anything, sweetheart, if it's in my power."

A flash of dimple betrayed that he wouldn't be daunted by her request. "I think it *must* be in your power," she said, "though sometimes I've begun to doubt it. What I want is a very simple thing: always to find you beside me when morning comes."

For a moment, he didn't comprehend the significance of what she was asking. Then a smile broke over his features, transforming him into her lover of the Breton coast.

"Is that all?" he asked joyfully.

Her own blue eyes gleaming at him from beneath long dark lashes, Rachel nodded. "Maybe it doesn't seem like much," she admitted, "but it means the earth to me. Haven't you guessed, my darling Marcus, how much I love you, too?"

In answer, his mouth covered hers. Like a man who has been starving and is suddenly presented with a banquet, he ran his hands over her body, glorying in its shape beneath the sensuous satin pajamas and reaching inside them to touch her skin.

Shivers of pleasure coursed through her, opening the place inside her heart that had been his since they'd come together the first time in his giant four-poster bed.

"Oh, yes . . . yes . . . yes," she prodded. "Please . . . make love to me, Marcus. I've wanted you so!"

Burning up with desire, he drew back to look at her. "Are you sure it's all right?" he asked. "It's only a month, or perhaps a little longer, since you've given birth."

Knowing how much he wanted her, Rachel feathered his mouth with blunt little kisses. "It's been all right, my darling. For several weeks," she answered.

He simply looked at her with love.

"I have protection," he eventually said, reaching into his pocket. "I want us to have more babies, but not just yet. First we have to finish our honeymoon."

Tenderly undressing her and then taking off his own things, he lay down with her on the couch. "Will that pillow be all right for your head?" he asked.

"Yes, it's perfect," she said.

Oh, she was thinking, just to feel him this way again! I must be the happiest woman in the world.

For his part, as he caressed each tender hollow and prepared to enter her, Marcus feared he couldn't last. He had wanted her too badly for that, he knew. During all those nights they had slept together, with their son in his crib beside them, she had burned in his blood like a fever. Day after day in his office, he'd dreamed of making love to her and felt his control go weak.

Instinctively guessing the cause of his hesitation, Rachel dared to invite him with her hands. "Please..." she whispered. "If it's over too quickly, we can do it again."

Their coupling was like an explosion. The conflagration that had been avoided on the runway that afternoon blazed up between them, fusing their bodies with the white heat of longing, then freeing them with the release they craved.

Later, tingling with afterglow, he covered her. They were separate again, yet in some deep way he understood completely but couldn't explain, he was more a part of her than ever.

Holding him, Rachel felt as if she'd burned to ashes. Yet she was a phoenix, too, rising up as if she could float above the world.

For a long time they were oblivious to the passage of time and to anything but each other. Neither noticed when the elderly butler looked in to see if they needed anything and smiled philosophically as he shut the door.

Whispering confidences, Marcus told her how difficult it had been for him, the press of business notwithstanding, to stay away from her so many lonely months.

"I struggled like a fiend against my emotions," he confessed, amazed at how easy it was now to tell her everything that was in his heart. "All along it would have been so easy... just to come home and make love to you the way I have this afternoon."

Gently Rachel kissed his shoulder. "Those weren't bad times," she insisted, "if they brought us together, made us appreciate the fact that we're the luckiest people alive."

Just then the phone rang. The study line was a private one and Marcus got up to answer it. Magnificently naked, he stood beside his desk to bark "no comment" concerning the day's mishap to an enterprising reporter who had somehow ferreted out his unpublished number.

They looked at each for a long moment as he put down the receiver, their thoughts connecting without words. Covering themselves so as not to scandalize the servants, they returned to their bedroom to check on their son. Together they leaned over his crib, marveling in hushed tones at his tiny perfect features, the wonder of his soft breathing, the delicate dark fringe his eyelashes made against one rosy cheek.

"Making love on the couch was wonderful, like what we did in the meadow full of flowers that afternoon in Brittany," Rachel said as they straightened, free to entice him now that she was sure of his love. "And later, that big tub I used to bathe in can stand in for the surf. But what about the haystack? I think I liked loving you there best of all."

Marcus rewarded her with a delighted grin. "We'll go back to Brittany tomorrow, if that would please you, my love," he said. "But for tonight, I have a plan."

Puzzled, she watched as he moved two heavily upholstered armchairs alongside their bed, then stripped off his shirt and shorts. Quickly though, as he climbed up on one of the chairs and invited her to mount the other, she delighted in his intent.

Carefully positioning themselves, at his signal they jumped onto the deep plush coverlet, to tumble laughing into each other's arms. In his nearby crib Jonathan whimpered, then found his thumb. He didn't wake as his parents set a second seal on their reconciliation.

Much later, when all but the last hint of daylight had faded, Marcus shook his head at his "damnably fine luck."

"With my bloody research and cracked-brain plan to get an heir, I could have saddled myself with anyone," he acknowledged. "Instead, I was fortunate enough to find you. I plan to show my appreciation by making certain we're not separated again."

"And when you must travel?" Rachel asked lazily from the shelter of his arms.

"I'll take you with me," he replied. "You *and* your precious baby."

"Perhaps for a while," she responded, putting him to the test. "But—difficult as it is to believe now— Jonathan will grow up someday, to wear Band-Aids on his knees and go off to nursery school. And there'll be other children...."

Shrugging, Marcus nibbled at her ear. From the perspective he had gained that afternoon, nothing would prove that difficult.

"When that time comes," he promised, "I'll rearrange my business affairs. Never doubt that I mean to keep you close beside me, Rachel. You're going to find this man in your bed every morning after the sun is up, for the rest of our long and happy life together."

\*     \*     \*     \*     \*

## WAYS TO *UNEXPECTEDLY* MEET MR. RIGHT:

♡ *Go out with the sexy-sounding stranger your daughter secretly set you up with through a personal ad.*

♡ *RSVP yes to a wedding invitation—soon it might be your turn to say "I do!"*

♡ *Receive a marriage proposal by mail— from a man you've never met....*

*These are just a few of the unexpected ways that written communication leads to love in Silhouette Yours Truly.*

*Each month, look for two fast-paced, fun and flirtatious Yours Truly novels (with entertaining treats and sneak previews in the back pages) by some of your favorite authors—and some who are sure to become favorites.*

## YOURS TRULY™:
*Love—when you least expect it!*

# FIVE UNIQUE SERIES
# FOR EVERY WOMAN YOU ARE...

 ROMANCE™

From classic love stories to romantic comedies to emotional heart tuggers, Silhouette Romance is sometimes sweet, sometimes sassy—and always enjoyable! Romance—the way you always knew it could be.

## SILHOUETTE® *Desire* ®

Red-hot is what we've got! Sparkling, scintillating, *sensuous* love stories. Once you pick up one you won't be able to put it down...only in Silhouette Desire.

## *Silhouette* SPECIAL EDITION®

Stories of love and life, these powerful novels are tales that you can identify with—romances with "something special" added in! Silhouette Special Edition is entertainment for the heart.

## SILHOUETTE·INTIMATE·MOMENTS®

Enter a world where passions run hot and excitement is always high. Dramatic, larger than life and always compelling—Silhouette Intimate Moments provides captivating romance to cherish forever.

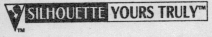

A personal ad, a "Dear John" letter, a wedding invitation... Just a few of the ways that written communication unexpectedly leads Miss Unmarried to Mr. "I Do" in Yours Truly novels...in the most fun, fast-paced and flirtatious style!

## LOOK FOR OUR FOUR FABULOUS MEN!

Each month some of today's bestselling authors bring
four new fabulous men to Harlequin American Romance.
Whether they're rebel ranchers, millionaire power brokers
or sexy single dads, they're all gallant princes—and
they're all ready to sweep you into lighthearted fantasies
and contemporary fairy tales where anything is possible
and where all your dreams come true!

You don't even have to make a wish...Harlequin American
Romance will grant your every desire!

Look for Harlequin American Romance wherever Harlequin
books are sold!

# Steven Spielberg
# and
# Amy Irving

Spielberg's first marriage was to actress Amy Irving. They had a son before they divorced.

He then became involved with actress Kate Capshaw. She met Spielberg when she auditioned for *Indiana Jones and the Temple of Doom*. She recalls that she intended the meeting as a seduction, not an interview. "I was determined not to ask about *E.T.* I kept asking somewhat personal questions. I was interested in who he was, not in getting the part. Here was my one chance to talk to Steven Spielberg, and I wasn't going to waste it trying to get a job." She got the part and a relationship developed. They had been together ten years, and had one child and another on the way when they got married.

B-SPIEL